This novel's story and characters are fictitious. Certain long-standing institutions, agencies, and public offices are mentioned, but the characters involved are wholly imaginary.

For my daughter Sahara who inspired me to create Sahara O'Malley. Brilliance, guts and dedication.

PREFACE

Sahara's Miracle is the second part of a trilogy of books that tell the multi-generational story of the O'Malley family.

The first book, Brian's Stolen Dream, tells the story of Brian and Parminder O'Malley and how Parminder helps Brian overcome the horrors of his childhood and realize his dream of the perfect family. Together, through a unique bond, they reach their dream despite facing the challenges of bigotry, racism and terrorism. Just as their life reaches the harmony they desire and their children are growing up, Brian is pulled down by his heritage and his legacy.

In a final act of violence, the IRA took Brian's life. Sahara's Miracle picks up from that horrific event.

THIS PAGE IS INTENTIONALLY BLANK

A Cold Reality

It's funny, it's said that burying a child is the greatest heart break a person can experience in life. Well, as Parminder stands in the quickly muddying dirt, holding an umbrella with her two children clasped tightly on each side of her, she might be excused for disagreeing.

The pain of watching that wooden casket slowly slip down beneath the earth while her two weeping children hold onto their one remaining parent, that parent might think they've successfully crossed the river Hades.

When you bury a child, with all its grief and sorrow, you retain a partner who ultimately may help you get through the pain and perhaps even one day, heal. Inevitably when a parent dies, the one left behind faces the understandable but inevitable barrage of 'what are we going to do now?' The challenge with that of course is there is no good answer, no one sits down in life and creates contingency plans for such an event, and even if they did, odds are they would fall miserably short in the harsh face of reality.

Yes, what the hell was she going to do? Parminder was brilliant but academically brilliant. Brian knew life and how to maneuver its corners and challenges, he was her man, he watched over her and the children and if need be could be counted on to step in and protect them. He was really gone now.

She did know Brian still watched over them, along with Parminder's mother. While it provided a comforting thought and it was in a spiritual capacity which would benefit them in the long run, that wasn't her immediate concern. It was the short run that worried Parminder. Yes, what was she going to do without Brian Parminder thought?

The funeral and the ceremony that followed were wonderfully delivered, with the precision of Swiss clockwork. As expected, it was well attended by both the area police forces and fire fighters. Parminder reflected on how the boys in blue were always so ready to stand up for a fallen comrade, too bad they were not so good when their comrade was still standing.

So, as they drove home, settled into the back of the limo so graciously provided by the police force, Parminder stared out through the raindrop covered window and reflected on life with the tears of her two children as a backdrop.

In a morbid mood, she could not be otherwise, she had lost her true love. 'So that's it, a life passed, just like that, in a single day, in a single moment.' She mused about how it was not unlike a wedding, a single day, a single moment.

Yes, life passes, fades away to grey carrying all its glory, sorrows, triumphs and failures with it. That's it, one day you're here, in vivid color, the next you're a shade like those who danced brightly in their own turn and reached their own end. Finally, you pack up your hopes and dreams as they alone will accompany you into the dirt Parminder morbidly realized.

Life as Usual

So, there it was, with the funeral passed, Parminder's new life began. It was not one anyone would have chosen for themselves, but one's life itself dictated in this case.

She was Indian, she could live with a life of hardship. In many ways, Indian women are prepared for this from youth. She knew that. In one of the cultural norms that should have outlived itself generations ago, Indian woman are expected to be martyrs, and prepared for it.

If it was just Parminder, well, she could cope, but the issue was the children. In many ways, with Brian gone, they were adrift in an ocean of growing ugliness. The war on terror wasn't making America any safer, it was making it more divided and Parminder and her kids were on the wrong side of the color bar.

Arriving back home, Brian's home, gray door and all, the falling rain seemed perfectly fitting for such a somber moment.

For the first time in her adult life, she missed her Indian family. Yes, even beyond her cherished mother. The idea of having an adult family around you in times of need was not so bad at that point as she stood, in some ways totally alone, before the gray soul entrance to their home. A home that was incomplete without its heart, Brian.

This she thought is where the next chapter of their life begins. The three of them huddled, in tears, on the couch, silently remembering better days while being equally worried about the future.

Suddenly the phone rang and pulled them, thankfully, out of the moment.

"Parm, how are you doing?" Jennifer asked. For Parminder the voice was that of an angel.

"Were okay." she replied, almost cursing herself for following into the martyr routine. Of course, they weren't okay, who would be? They had just buried the most important man in their lives.

Jennifer also recognized this and knew this was a time where Parminder needed a gift, so, as her best friend, Jennifer was about to give her one.

"Parm, I know that's not true, let me help. I need to for my own heart. I'm on my way to pick you guys up. Pack a light bag, I've booked a place out of town for the next three nights for the four of us, don't argue." Jennifer replied with a stern tone, only to ensure Parminder complied.

While in different times, Parminder would have put up a light defense, at minimum, offered to pay, but this wasn't that time, she simply complied; Jennifer she thought was indeed a true friend.

So Parminder told the children, who were quite happy at the prospect of a break from the empty home. It just felt wrong, at least right now, to be there, without Brian. They would have to get used to it eventually, just not today.

Jennifer came by an hour later, grabbed the three of them and in a simple act lifted their souls.

She had booked a place in Cape Cod, a perfect fall getaway.

"Jennifer, I can't thank you enough. Frankly, we didn't realize how much we needed this escape." Parminder said, truly feeling the emotion in her as they approached Cape Cod and its natural beauty.

Parminder loved her home, it was the only the home the children had ever known but given the situation, Cape Cod was just the right thing.

"Parm, remember, I've seen my own share of painful moments." Jennifer replied.

Of course, she had Parminder remembered. Jennifer had lost both her parents some years back. Then it was Parminder's turn to provide support, a private smile between the two was all that was needed.

Jennifer had booked a quaint little cottage near the seaside, perfect for the four of them to get their bearings and spirits back.

"Mom, are we really staying here?" Sahara cheered from the back.

"You bet we are." was Jennifer's answer to which Sahara and Dylan both erupted in cheer.

As Jennifer and Parminder worked the lock box on the door, the children ran around back and all that could be heard was more cheering.

"Jennifer, I can't thank you enough. In three hours, the kids had gone from somber tears to cheering and seeing that brings my own heart up, more so than I thought would be possible." Parminder said, expressing the warmth in her heart.

Once the adults figured out the complexity of the lock box, the crew checked out the cottage. They were all excited about the weekend to come.

An Update from the New World

Kieran felt a little more comfortable about his pending call with Conor than he had the last time. True, he had killed a cop and a priest, in a church on top of that, but that was part of the job and it was done quietly, unlike his church explosion fiasco. His Irish bosses would be okay with that, he was quite certain. As he himself had said, they were the IRA, not the Vatican.

Now, was God okay with that? Well, Kieran had known for a long time where he was headed upon his own death. For him God's opinion was meaningless. He knew he would be serving a different master when his time came.

Finally, the phone rang. Okay, let's get this bloody thing going "Kieran here." he started, ready for anything. In the end the call did go reasonably well, certainly better than last time. Brian's death was being played into a bigger scenario of Muslim copycat terrorist, with the help of the Boston police, simplified by the fact that the FBI had backed out.

More importantly for Kieran, he wanted to try and find out when the hell he was he going to be released from his purgatory in Boston and get back to his county Kerry.

As the call was about to end, Kieran broached the subject, "Conor, with the cop and the priest out of the way, and the money moving again, when do I get back to Ireland?"

"Kieran, I don't want to make this sound like a punishment, but maybe it is. We're going to keep you there for a little longer, until we're sure that the church incident is bloody well behind us." Conor spoke. Slow and purposeful, to ensure his message and authority were understood.

Bloody right, it was a punishment thought Kieran. He knew Conor pretty well and knew the tactics even better. To be fair, he expected this. Conor knew Kieran's dislike of America and keeping him there a little longer was clearly how Conor was sending his message.

Call done, Kieran settled back into his Ikea couch and closed his eyes with the image of the ring of Kerry in his head, a momentary release from this unpleasant new world.

Okay, enough escape, back to business. He picked up the phone and dialed Kevin's number. He needed to make sure his little prodigy wasn't having second thoughts.

A Pleasant Break

The four of them had their little tea party, a Boston tea party, and like four school kids at their first tea party, they had a great time.

It seemed even the weather gods had decided to give the family a break. The clouds and rain of the funeral had given way to sun and mild temperatures.

They awoke early each day, shared making and eating breakfast together, followed by a waterfront walk. Afternoons were mild enough for Parminder and Jennifer to sit in the backyard and share a wine, or two or three as the case may be.

The kids kept themselves amused in the gardens and in the little nooks and crannies of the cottage neighborhood.

Dinners, like breakfasts, they all shared the task of preparing. Even Dylan participated but he was quietly given the simpler tasks. When the dinners were ready, they would bypass the traditional dinner table for dining on the coffee table in the large main room, with a full fire going. More than once, a child or two needed to be carried to bed.

On the last night, kids in bed, Parminder and Jennifer had some quiet time to reflect upon life.

"Jennifer, pardon the question, but given what has just happened, it's forefront in my thoughts, did you ever get past your parents death?" Parminder asked, referring of course to Jennifer's parents who had died in a commuter plane accident almost twenty years ago, on their way to come to visit Jennifer.

Parminder waited for some sign of pain in Jennifer's face. She hated the thought of forcing her best friend to revisit that episode of her life, but as she was about to really start dealing with Brian's death, she needed to let her know that there was hope in letting go.

Jennifer had lost her own mother years ago in that accident, but in a strange way, despite the importance of her mother, she was eventually able to accept that.

Parminder had a deep spiritual connection with her own mother still to this day, something she had never shared even with Jennifer. No, Brian was the only one that knew that story.

The fact was that she, in many ways, said goodbye to her mother all those years ago, as the train, slowly pulled its way out of the station in the north of India. Pulling her out of one life and into another.

Jennifer did not show the pain Parminder had expected. In fact, she almost showed a look of content contemplation.

"Parm, I will say you never fully get over it, and yes the first years are the hardest, but in the end, I found a place where I enjoy the memories I shared with them and happiness for the time we had together." Jennifer replied.

With that answer Parminder smiled, at least for the time being. Jennifer curled over and held Parminder in a warm hug, just as they had done so many years ago when they were young and innocent.

The next morning it seemed that God had decided the break was over, the cloud gathered on the horizon and by the time they were ready to leave, the rains had rejoined their life.

Just before leaving, Parminder grabbed Jennifer and hugged her with all her heart and soul. The weekend gave her just enough, she knew, to get through the challenge ahead.

Second Thoughts

While Kevin sat in a local dive bar, waiting for Kieran, his head was all over the place.

What the hell had he done? While he didn't pull the trigger on that last shot, he had in effect killed Brian and for what? A cause thousands of miles away.

Yes, he was Irish, all the lads from his neighborhood were. Sure they had heard the stories growing up but shit, this wasn't a story anymore, it was a living nightmare.

He hadn't slept well for days. Every time he closed his eyes, he saw Brian's face, in those last minutes and worst, Brian's wife and kids. He also had scenes from the many Thanksgiving events at Brian's house, a guest of Brian's generosity, and how did he repay him, with a bullet.

Suddenly he saw Kieran walk in. Okay, time to toughen up he thought. He knew he could not show any remorse or weakness, that was suicide in the eyes of men like Kieran.

No, he had better shape up real fast or he would be having a reunion with Brian.

He watched as Kieran made his way into the bar, better yet, as he waltzed through the bar to the tune of his own song. He was alpha, the lion no matter where he was. Kevin wondered what deal with the devil the man had made to carry so much power, better yet, to carry no remorse in life.

Kieran made his way to Kevin, "Kevin. Let's grab a seat in the corner." Kieran said, sounding a little more like an order than an ask.

They took a place in the back corner, well out of the reach of listening ears and Kieran started his inquisition.

"So, Kevin, all is good?" he asked.

There was one of those questions that had only one right answer. "Yeah, I'm good." Kevin replied.

He hoped it had come out strong, he had been practicing it all day since he got the call from Kieran.

Kevin watched as Kieran sized him up, waiting patiently to see if he had passed the test. For a few, very long seconds, Kieran looked over Kevin, then he suddenly patted him heartily on the back and said, "Of course you are lad, of course you are."

"Kevin, you're part of the resistance now, you're playing your part in the bigger picture for a better Ireland." Kieran said, with what seemed to Kevin to be an elaborated Irish accent.

"You know that comes with some expectations and more importantly an ongoing commitment to the cause." Kieran continued.

That Kevin thought, that was exactly what he was worried about.

Kevin started to think about the situation again, how easily it was to get into it, how hard it was to get out.

Once again, he steadied himself and responded "Kieran, you know I'm with the cause, I've done more than any of the guys at the station."

Again, Kieran looked him over, sizing up his answer, the man was clearly an expert at it, this time, he took a little longer look.

What Kevin didn't know, was that this was a standard process for Kieran. He had spent a better part of a lifetime doing this. He was a master at sizing and intimidating people, he did both effectively in one shot.

"That's true Kevin, we have that little secret together don't we?" he finally said.

For Kevin the thought of sharing a dark secret with an IRA fixer was not at the top of his list, but he knew, he had put himself in this spot. In fairness, there weren't good options available at the time. The other option was the path Brian took and well that one was arguably worse.

The real issue was higher up the chain of command, people like Brian and Kevin were just pawns in a much bigger chess game.

The two of them finished their beers off with some mindless chit chat, the purpose of the meeting had already been achieved. Kieran had assessed Kevin's mindset and re-established enough fear in him to keep him quiet. If they were to meet again, it would be a more typical Kieran meeting and it would be Kevin's last on earth.

As Kevin drove home, he felt he had just dodged a bullet, the fact was he had.

Another Unwelcome Homecoming

Some part of Parminder expected to come home to something off. She almost felt guilty about having such a wonderful weekend, she was after all a Punjabi Sikh woman. It was her duty to mourn, it was built into her genetics, engrained through guilty So, they pulled up to the house, much like they had that day after her honeymoon, the mood just as crushed.

Seeing the message on the door, Parminder almost chuckled to herself, "Fuck you Muslims!" Funny enough, they were closer to reality the first time around with go home Paki. She was Sikh, much closer to Paki than Muslim.

This was the new America; those distinctions didn't matter. She was waiting for the children to comment and was only mildly surprised when neither one said anything. They too were apparently now numb to the racism that was sweeping the country.

"Parm, you know I can come by tomorrow, we can repaint that door." Jennifer said, knowing in her own heart that this was a much different situation to that last time.

"Thank you, Jennifer, but you know, I think this time were not going to do anything." Parminder replied, as she watched for the children's reaction, again, nothing. That was a little concerning to Parminder, but then again, they had just lost their father.

Jennifer understood, this was the moment for her to let the grieving family have their time. She was happy for the gift she was able to give them, in some ways it was repaying

Parminder for a similar gift from years ago, but more so it was because she wanted to. With a nod and a hug Jennifer set the family free.

Once again, they passed through that gateway into the home. It was like the clouds had gathered once again, the Cape Cod weekend was quickly a memory and it was back to reality. Now it was time for Parminder to mourn, yes, part of it was cultural, but the biggest part was simply human. She missed Brian and her heart truly ached.

In the end the decision to leave the door as is was seemed to have surprised the neighborhood. While most of the neighbors were not bad people, it's easy to fall in line with the general society mindset. Just ask any German in the mid 1930s.

Honoring Her Father's Legacy

For Sahara, the O'Malley island was the heart of what family values should be. It was the altar, the speak easy, and many times also the dinner table. It was built from her father's family dream with many loving hours from the four of them and, as such, reflected her father's spirit.

As Sahara stood in the dark, looking over the island, partially rebuilt from damage inflicted on it by both the church explosion and her father's rage, she felt a large gap in her own spirit. She knew what she needed to do, she need to complete the island rebuild, for her father, for her, in fact for all four of them.

So, one Saturday morning, just as her father had done years before, she dragged her mother and brother down into the basement. For Parminder, it was somewhat uncomfortable. She had not been in the basement since Brian had passed. Too many bad spirits for her, it was Brian's lair, during his difficult time and as such held an image for Parminder that was not the Brian she loved but if there was any reason to go down there, Sahara's request was it.

Once downstairs, Sahara led them to the island and started, "Family, this is O'Malley island." at which Parminder looked upon her daughter in some degree of awe. She really had the ability to create a presence and hold attention, it was her powerful confidence.

She thought about her own mother, a brilliant, wonderful person, then herself, arguably even more brilliant than her mother, but both lived with the limitation of a traditional Indian woman upbringing.

Here was Sahara, gifted with perhaps an even greater intellect than both of them, but with none of the shackles.

"This was Dad's dream and I believed in it too, just as you did Mom and you did Dylan. With Dad gone, I think we should finish the rebuild in his honor." Sahara continued.

There was a pause, Sahara was not expecting a pause, for her there should be no question about the importance of this.

For Parminder she understood why Sahara felt this way. In fact, she did too but for her, there was a degree of pain that accompanied being in the basement, around the island, it was a reminder for her of the loss.

For Dylan, he loved the island because the four of them spent time together and were free from the world's challenges. In his mind, with his father gone, it simply wasn't the same.

Parminder started almost with tears in her eyes, much because of the mixed emotion in her "Sahara, what a lovely idea, yes, perhaps we could work on this."

Dylan continued "I guess so, but it doesn't feel the same without Dad."

Sahara was upset at both their answers, she had expected a clear runway, more than that, she expected support.

Sahara thought about it for a few seconds, she had two choices, keep pressing or take the initiative herself. While she had hoped that her family would jump in, she was also prepared to do it alone. As she analyzed her own family, one thought, a mature one for her age, that hit her was that each one of them was dealing with Brian's death in their own way. She knew what she needed to do.

"Okay I'll get it started and then we can all work together." was her final answer.

Over the next few weeks Sahara did just that. Every day after school, she was downstairs, working on her father's spirit.

One day, her brother came down and was amazed at how far Sahara had gotten and suddenly felt a little guilty for not helping. He rolled up his sleeves and joined in, which he also continued to do every day after school from then on. While the island continued to grow, more importantly so did the bond between the two of them.

While the two of them always had a good relationship, it was based somewhat on Sahara looking after her brother. Here they were as actual equals, and both thoroughly enjoyed their time together.

Unknown to either of them, was just how much they needed each other, to fill the void left with the loss of their father.

One day, when they felt the time was right, they invited their mother downstairs to show her what they had done. Parminder agreed, despite her uneasy feeling with the basement, she made her way down and was so happy in the end that she did. What the children had done was amazing, in particular Sahara, the island was a true honor to her father.

She suddenly also realized that she herself had pulled away from the children, unintentionally, likely as she herself was still mourning in her private way.

Tears began to well up in her eyes and she hugged both of her children. "Sahara and Dylan, what you have done is wonderful and your father would have loved it. I have only one question. Any chance we could bring the island upstairs?" Parminder asked.

Sahara, understanding her mother's discomfort with the basement quickly replied "Of course."

A Painful Cover-up

As Kevin sat in the daily police briefing, he listened with a heavy heart.

The latest news from the investigation was that there were some bad cops shaking down the local churches for protection money and were working with local Islamic groups as the scare tactic.

They officially announced that Brian was one of the cops and was killed in a dispute over money.

Kevin knew the truth, worse yet, he knew the role he had played in Brian's death, something he so very much wished he could now undo.

Once back at his desk, a couple of the guys came by "Hey, you used to work with Brian. Did you catch that today? Why do you think he went that way? I heard he had gambling debts." one of them said.

The other one piped in "I heard he got caught up in his wife's Muslim group and their fight."

As Kevin sat there listening, his heart twisted even further down. Knowing the truth, knowing that Brian was in fact a good man. That he himself was the one that fell, not Brian, and for what, a cause that he frankly never really understood. No in fact that was the cover story, he fell because he was weak, like so many of his colleagues.

"Brian's wife isn't Muslim, she is Sikh." Kevin said, not entirely sure why he did, for Brian's memory or for his own conscience.

"Same thing." his colleague replied.

Same thing, even Kevin started to see the issue in that. He was no race relation expert, but he at least understood there were differences within the ethnic groups and not recognizing that the "same thing" mindset was dangerous, well at least for those people it was.

What really started to get to Kevin was the thought of Brian's family. He knew times were already tough for Parminder and her family. When this news got out, things were most likely to go downhill for them even further.

Suddenly, he really didn't feel good about where he was in life.

Difficult Decisions

One thing that Brian did, similar to what his father did when Brian was younger, was to ensure that both his children had the ability to defend themselves.

Remembering the experience of the boxing, he had recognized that was not the right fit for his kids and given the evolution of self-defense he chose a more modern and effective method, Brazilian Jujitsu.

While both children were comfortable with the training, it was Sahara who stepped up and in fact was one of the tops in the program. Again, there was something in her that drove her to compete in all aspects of life.

Dylan enjoyed it as well but simply did not have the competitive nature that his sister had.

So, one afternoon as the family was just starting to work back into regular life, Dylan got jumped on his way back from school.

For some reason, despite his training, he simply elected not to fight back. The fight was of course related to culture, as it was years ago and just like she did the first time around, Sahara stepped in and defended her brother, very effectively.

On the way home, Sahara asked her brother a critical question. "Dylan, you're just as trained as I am. Why didn't you defend yourself?"

"I'm not sure. I guess it's because I'm not sure if Dad would have been happy with me hurting someone." was

Dylan's response, which spoke volumes to what was in his heart, the emotion that managed his life.

"Dylan, Dad put us through that training. He wanted us to be able to defend ourselves, in fact he would have been upset knowing you didn't protect yourself." Sahara responded.

"Remember years ago, when you were attacked and I helped you? What did Dad do? He went into the school and yelled at the principle and then found BJJ training for us." she said.

Dylan thought about it for a moment and he started to connect the dots. Although sometimes people didn't fight because they were scared, that wasn't the case for Dylan.

His fear wasn't fighting, his fear was being found in the wrong. He was more emotionally driven than physically driven and his sister's message was getting through.

"Sahara, you really think that?" he questioned her. She replied very quickly and very directly.

"Dylan, I know it. I won't be around every time and I would feel really bad if something happened to you because I wasn't there." she said.

Well that one hit the spot, she saw him change at that moment. They were both thirteen and as is quite common for children, even twins, he had now become bigger than her.

"You know what Sahara, your right. I'm not going to let that happen again." Dylan replied, with confidence.

"Okay, cool, now let's talk about what we tell Mom. She's got a lot on her mind, so I suggest we just keep this one quiet." Sahara said to which Dylan simply nodded yes, he was still working some things out in his head.

Once home, they cleaned Dylan up and waited for their mother. No word of the incident was spoken.

The next week, on a day when the school kids knew Sahara was in an after-school event, the same two boys that had attacked Dylan the week before were waiting for him.

"Hey, Bin Laden, where's your sister today?" one of the white kids asked.

Dylan, with honesty, as it was his way, answered "She has debate club after school today."

The two boys chuckled with each other and then circled Dylan.

"Well, I guess you are on your own then Bin Laden." With that one of the boys jumped him but this time, Dylan was emotionally free to defend himself.

The two boys, well that day one could say, learned what could be called a lesson of a lifetime. When the first one grabbed him, Dylan went into full BJJ mode, flipped him and pulled him down on top of himself and put him into a sleeper hold, within five seconds the first one was out.

With that Dylan pushed the unconscious boy off of him and went after the second boy. He quickly tackled him and put him in an arm bar and ignored the boy's pleads to stop and continued to pull until the boy's arm broke.

He then patiently got up, collected his bag and walked home.

When Parminder got home she had a very disturbing call from the school. After listening she gathered Dylan and also Sahara.

"Dylan what happened today?" Parminder asked to which Dylan answered, "I decided to fight back."

Sahara got up and hugged Dylan and said, "About time."

A little piece of Parminder felt like doing the same thing but she realized that the situation was quite serious this time as one of the boys was hospitalized.

"Dylan, while I think it's good that you have stood up for yourself, unfortunately one of the boys has been hospitalized with a severely broken arm." Parminder said.

"We will have to see the principle tomorrow and the other boys' parents." She continued. "They have agreed to keep the police out it for now."

With the children in bed, Parminder settled in with a Chai, she needed a momentary break. The Chai still gave the emotional escape it always did, but lately it made her think about Brian. In many ways his bottle wasn't that different, it gave him his escape, she suddenly felt a degree of guilt.

The difference was of course that the Chai didn't drive another one and another one and another one. No, this escape was simple and natural, but in the end, not entirely different, we all have our addictions she thought.

Later that night, as Parminder was roaming the fields of the Punjab in her mind, the phone rang and instantly Parminder was flown thousands of miles out of the warm, breezy tall grasses of her childhood home to reality, her house, grey door and all in Boston. "Parm, it's Shane, glad I caught you. A friend down at the station just called, apparently they're implying Brian was part of a group that was shaking down the local churches and that's what got him killed." Shane told her.

Parminder sat momentarily in shock, her moral compass was spinning, they kill the love of her life and now they're going to kill his image.

"Shane, no one can possibly believe this." was Parminder's first response. Entirely emotional, entirely true, but this was a new America, truth was secondary to personal objectives.

"Parm, we both know it's not about the truth anymore. I'm worried about you and the kids and I'm sure there will be some fallout from this." Shane continued.

Some fallout, Parminder was still processing Shane's first comment. Suddenly visions of the long grass, moving like waves in a warm sea, of her birth home filled her again. Yes, this new world offered so much opportunity, but at what cost, it's the cost part that no one computes into their dreams.

She remembered one trip she took as a youngster, to Zanzibar, with her family to visit relatives. At the end of the first day in Stone town, they went down to the port where everyone gathered at the end of the day. There were food stalls and entertainment, but more so there were people happy with life, singing and chanting. They were happy with next to nothing, they didn't need a new phone, a new bike or a new car, they just needed each other.

She remembered watching, how they were not that different from the people of her village in culture and history but very different in disposition.

Dreams she knew were ultimately created when one faced a gap in the fulfillment of their life, simple as that she thought.

In her case, there was no question while in India, working in the fields of the farm or using the brain that God gave her, the dream was the only path for her life.

The next day, they all put on their best looks and went down to the school, expecting a not so enjoyable meeting which, in fact is exactly what they got.

The presence of the other family there was hard. An Irish family from the neighborhood and it didn't take long for Parminder to understand where the boy in question got the racism, straight down from father to son.

"The problem we got here is that we got too many immigrants." The boy's father started, fortunately the principal cut him off early.

"George, the problem we have here is your boy and his friends have been picking on Dylan for a while now. What Dylan did was wrong but what the boys did was too. What I'm going to do is suspend Dylan for a week and suspend the other boys for 3 days."

Of course, George protested but, kudos to the principal he stuck to his guns. He was new this year and was setting the bar high. Parminder appreciated that, at least someone was viewing the situation without the use of a color bar.

"We understand principal Lacroix, the one week is reasonable." Parminder replied. She then looked down at Dylan who nodded.

On the way out the door, George confronted Parminder. "You know what, you darkies need to go back to your own country, we didn't have problems like this when it was just us folks here."

The funny thing, and Parminder was tempted to inform George of it, was that the same was said about the Irish a number of years back, people just naturally resisted change, fear of the unknown.

After a moment of thought, she realized it would only antagonize him further, she made her way towards the car. Just as she was about to get in, George fired his final volley, and it was a painful one "It's people like you that turn good men like your husband into criminals and that's where your kids are headed."

Parminder quickly got herself and Dylan into the car and headed home.

"Mom, what did he mean about Dad being a criminal, he was wrong wasn't he?" Dylan asked, very emotionally.

This was exactly what Parminder feared the most about the story Shane had told her, the impact on the children, especially Dylan.

She thought about her response, realizing the weight it was going to carry and then responded, "Yes Dylan, he was completely wrong. Simply look at the man and his nature compared to your father and you can plainly see that."

She waited for a moment, watching for signs from Dylan, she could sense him mulling it over. Fortunately it wasn't long, "I thought so Mom." was his response. Good enough for now but Parminder knew she had a brewing problem to address.

Well as soon as she got home, she realized the problem wasn't brewing, it was here. Sahara was sitting on the couch and crying. "Mom, some people at school are saying that Dad was a crook." Sahara managed to say between weeps.

Dylan, interestingly, sat down with his sister and hugged her. He said, "Someone at school said that to us too, Mommy told me it wasn't true."

Sahara suddenly recovered quickly and her sadness quickly turned to anger.

"Mom why would people lie like this?" she said with a real edge, "That's not right."

Parminder, took a deep breath and the three of them had a mature conversation about what was happening, surprisingly the children understood.

"So, Mom, this is what Dad was telling us before he died. There was another group and now that other group is blaming Dad." Sahara wisely said.

"That's effectively it Sahara." Parminder replied.

"Mom, we have to get that stopped, it's not fair to Dad." Dylan responded.

Parminder looked admirably at Dylan, he had so much of his father in him.

"It's not so simple Dylan but you're right. It's not fair to your father's image or reputation, but there is a system in America. It controls a lot of people, people that are much more powerful that your father was." Parminder replied, then she stopped to think about what she had just said.

It wasn't untrue, it was a complex issue and took an understanding of the structure of America, that frankly Parminder was still grasping, and only because she found herself in a situation where it significantly affected her life.

She took a moment to reflect upon her new home, the land of dreams for so many. Very few understand the reality of this new world. It had become successful because of its system, but it came at a cost, something Parminder was just beginning to fully understand.

She could see the confused looks on her children's faces and quickly added "That is something that you will not be able to fully understand at your age, but in time you will. I'll go to the police station tomorrow and have a discussion with them about this, but I will tell you, what started today will likely not stop. It's simply the way things work in this country."

"Mom, what are we going to do?" Sahara asked.

For Parminder, it was that question she walked away from the funeral with and the one she most feared. She had managed to avoid it in many ways to date, but in her heart, she knew she would have to deal with the bigger 'What are we going to do?" picture, which of course, was where they lived.

"Kids, what we really need to talk about is where we live. As you know this was your father's house before we got married. It's an old neighborhood and as you know it's not very multi-cultured, we might be better off in a different neighborhood, one that is more consistent with our background." Parminder started, but was cut off quickly by Sahara. "But this is our home, we were born here."

Parminder was reminded that what Sahara had said was in fact true. For her, she had lived in other places and in fact was born far away from this house but for the kids, this was their birth home, the one place they knew. Changing, no matter the situation, would be emotional.

"Sahara, that is true, but as was the case in my life there is a time for a change." Parminder replied.

With that the two kids fell into thought. Parminder reached over, gave them each a kiss and said, "Both of you should think about it, we will have to make a decision soon."

A few days later, after work, Parminder swung by the police station to speak to the Sergeant. She was received politely, but not with open arms, which is more common for the partner of a downed officer, but she could happily live with polite these days. After a bit of a wait, she was escorted to the Sergeant's office.

"Parminder, it's a pleasure to see you, I hope all is well." the sergeant said, and he stood and shook her hand.

"The three of us are physically fine, but there is something that is affecting us that I wanted to speak to you about." Parminder said and watched for the sergeant's face. Surprisingly no change, Brian had said he had a good poker face.

"Certainly Parminder, is it something we can help with?" he asked.

"Well, in some ways, yes. I have been told that the investigation into the church incident is suggesting that Brian was involved in something illegal. That information is making its way around the neighborhood and we have already had some repercussions." Parminder intentionally left the comment there, another opportunity to watch for a reaction. Again nothing, the man was good.

"Parminder, it's true that there is some evidence to suggest that but we have not made that an official statement. I can certainly understand how that might be upsetting news, we are doing our best to clarify the situation and to protect his reputation." the sergeant replied.

Well, Parminder then decided it was time for her trump card. She wasn't sure if she was going to do this when she walked in but something the way the sergeant was speaking, it just didn't sit right with Parminder.

"Perhaps you should also be following up on the IRA, as Brian was when he was killed. You do realize this is exactly the type of story the media outlets love." she said.

Parminder played her cards well. So much for the poker face, she watched as the man, who only moments before was in complete control, visibly struggling to maintain control.

"Mrs. O'Malley, you need to understand that is an unwise course of action. Our investigation, which I'm not at liberty to share, indicates no involvement of that group such as this. Involving the media will create more problems for you than you currently have, trust me." the sergeant finally spoke, clearly focused. With that they both clearly mentally decided to leave the line drawn where it was. With that she stood up and took her leave.

Once home, Parminder sat down with the children "I met with the sergeant today and it appears that there will not be much support for us. In fact, I do not believe I will meet with them again." she said at which Dylan leaned forward and hugged her then followed by Sahara.

"We will need to decide soon on what we should do in terms of living arrangements." Parminder continued.

"We know Mom, both Dylan and I heard about how Dad was a crook again today. But this time, no went near Dylan." Sahara smiled and turned to Dylan and gave him a high five, then they both smiled, to which Parminder in turn smiled.

One thing in her life that was a big blessing was the children, they were really growing up right and truly cared for each other, something that all parents dreamt about.

During the night, Sahara went to see Dylan. She had a dream. She told Dylan about. In the dream she was sitting in a backyard, not their current yard but a different one. She was sitting on an old woman's lap, something she had not done in years, but was happy.

She assumed she was younger in the dream; her mother was there and simply smiling as she watched Sahara with the old woman. The old woman whispered into Sahara's ear and said, "My dear, it's time to move." Just before the dream ended, she saw her father in the back window of the house and he looked at her and smiled.

Sahara told Dylan about the dream; he immediately understood the meaning.

"Sahara, I guess the message is that we need to move. I'm okay with that. I would like that in fact for Mom, she needs a change, this was Dad's house, but he's gone now." Dylan said.

Sahara reached forward and hugged him

So, the next morning, as the family sat down to discuss the future, Sahara told Parminder about the dream, to which Parminder smiled, "Sahara, you're connecting with my Mother, she's helping all of us." she said.

"Well Mom, she clearly wants us to move." Sahara replied.

Parminder already knew, her mother visited her earlier this week. "Dylan are you okay with this?" Parminder asked of Dylan.

He smiled and responded "Mom, anything that makes you happy I'm okay with."

Parminder, sitting on the couch with her two children, was suddenly back on O'Malley island.

To New Horizons

Parminder awoke and reflected upon her decision, well her family's decision. For her, this move was big but for the children it was even bigger. She knew that and thought about how mature they had become.

It's sad she thought, losing a parent inevitably creates significant changes in the lives of the children. In some cases, it's a negative. The child, unable to process the loss falls into a bad place and depending on the age of the child, that can be devastating.

In all cases, there are few greater changes in life for a child than losing a parent. How children react is generally the sum of the experience of the upbringing, the nature of the loss and how the remaining parent responds. In Parminder's case, whether she knew it or not, she was a rock.

The move of course would need to coincide with the start of the school year, so the family would have to put up with a few more months in their little hovel.

She recognized it would be a tough period, but they would have the benefit of knowing their time there had an expiry date.

The bigger question was where to go. A move across town was easier, but Parminder did not know how far reaching the church issue was. A move across country was safer but came at a cost. Parminder was well entrenched at Harvard and while she could find work at many universities across the country, she would have to rebuild herself there and re-establish what she had already built at Harvard.

The children of course would have an opinion. For them, a move across Boston was tough enough, a move across the country was a whole other thing.

She thought about the relatives she had in California. That was an option and there were certainly enough universities there. She knew if they did that they would be effectively living in an Indian community. She wasn't fully comfortable in an Indian environment given the decision she had made on marriage and her own upbringing.

If they stayed in Boston, they had the consideration of their family name. One option was to change to Gill from O'Malley, she hated the thought of that. While it might provide some distance from the current issue, it was in her mind disrespectful to Brian's memory.

She had so much to think about, she made her way to the kitchen, a Chai and a momentary escape.

That evening the family sat down to the biggest discussion of their life to date. A move is always more traumatic than anyone ever expects. Sure, it's just packing and driving to a new place. Yes, on the surface it is, but the truth is your home is a big part of your identity. It's a part of your past, your history and in many cases, it likely helped make you the person you are.

Much of this is often overlooked, but for Parminder she was very reflective of the issues. Her first thought was the old red door, a pleasant thought.

"Okay family O'Malley, we need to come to a decision on where we're going. There are many options but there are some things we should consider in making a decision. From my own experience, the most important consideration is understanding the reason for a move. In our case I believe that is based on a new start and putting the issues you two have and are facing at school behind us." Parminder started. She waited a moment, both kids were nodding in approval.

"Mom, if we're going to move, we should consider the type of home we want, and it must have a place for the island." Sahara added.

"Of course, Sahara." Parminder replied, respectful of the importance Sahara placed on the island. The image of her father's dream.

"We will find a home with a special place for the island." Parminder added.

From that point the family got into a sensible discussion about places to live. They were all, thankfully, in agreement about staying in Boston.

They knew a few neighborhoods that were closer to Harvard and with the money from the house, and a pension from the police and Parminder's salary, they could likely afford a decent place in one of them. So, it was done, they were going to move but stay in Boston. She decided to take down one challenge at a time, the last name discussion could wait.

As the discussion broke up, Sahara had one last request, "Mom, can we paint the door red?" They all laughed.

Jennifer had a friend who was a real estate agent and introduced Parminder to her. Sarah, she was an experienced rep and knew the neighborhoods Parminder was considering well.

"Have you thought about the schools in those neighborhoods? It's an important consideration." Sarah asked.

Parminder had done quite a bit of research. Each of the communities offered excellent options for schools, so the decision was going to come down to the choice of houses and the cultural makeup of the neighborhood.

So, the three of them, with Sarah's help spent a few weeks looking at houses until they found one bungalow. The layout was perfect, and it even had a nook in the living room for the island, but what sold it was the backyard. As soon as Sahara walked out into it, she turned to her mom, "Mom, this is it, this is the backyard from the dream." Sahara said and as she did she thought for a split second that she saw her father's reflection in the window and he was smiling.

After a week of showings, they received several offers. It seemed that there were plenty of people that felt they could fit into that old white neighborhood. From memory she didn't recall a single Indian family doing a visit. Parminder selected one offer, gave Sarah the instructions and then got the call she was waiting for, "Good news, we have a deal, lets close on the bungalow now."

So, there it was, a sold sign, just four letters but it carried such a significance to Parminder. Brian's death brought about the end to an important chapter in her life, the sold sign closed the book. On August 18, 2003, barely two years after 9/11 and less than a year from the loss of their father, the family started packing for their next book.

A New Concern for the Cause

Kieran hung up the phone, he had just had a disconcerting chat with sergeant Hynes.

He sat down on his Ikea couch, in the bland rental apartment and cursed, and cursed and cursed. To him it was starting to feel like déjà vu all over again. Brian's wife was threatening to make some waves. In Brian's father's case, they took care of her first, counted on the father falling apart, and it had turned out to be a good bet on their part.

This time around Brian had already fallen apart, but unlike his father he recovered. Killing the wife would have only opened up a big investigation and risk, as there was no sensible story they could tie to her. She was as clean as a whistle based on their research. The worst part was this likely meant he was stuck in Boston for even longer. His patience was running thin already, but as important as he was, he didn't call the shots.

He picked up the phone again and called Conor.

"What is it Kieran?" he snapped. He was either never in a good mood, or this was how he managed people.

Kieran had known him long enough to know it was the latter. "We might have a little complication with the wife." Kieran started and then went into the details. After a brief discussion Conor asked, "What do you suggest?"

Conor might be the man in charge, but he was wise enough to know that his guys on the ground understood the situation much better than he did.

Kieran explained his thinking on the wife and suggested that for the time being, they'll just monitor this situation. He added, "I have a plan if that doesn't work out, it deals with another potential problem that we might have down the line." He was speaking about Kevin.

When they met, Kevin might have thought he got a passing grade from Kieran, perhaps he did, but it was a D at best, just enough for a pass. Kieran knew the risk was not gone.

They agreed to stand tight, which for Kieran meant more time in Boston. He hung up the phone, sat down and closed his eyes and had visions of the ring of Kerry in his head and a brief smile passed across his face.

Some Unexpected Help

As the family packed up their home and their lives to start again, an unexpected visitor came by to help, Brian's old friend Shane.

The reality of moving is that one generally finds out they have significantly more stuff than they ever believed they did, as the O'Malley family was finding out, so any help was more than welcome.

"O'Malley family, a little bird told me you could use some help." Shane said as he stepped through the open door.

He hadn't been by in some time, the fact was he felt a little odd being around the family with Brian gone and he was dealing with his own personal issue, his marriage had fallen apart. But something told him today was the right time to step in, so he did.

"Shane, my God are we glad to see you, yes please roll up your sleeves and give us a hand, many thanks for coming." Parminder replied.

What neither was aware of is that Jennifer had worked some of her magic in making the connection happen. Shane was coming off a terrible breakup and had always had a good relationship with Parminder and well, Jennifer figured Parminder could use a little male company.

Shane more than rolled up his sleeves, he put his back and his heart into helping and frankly made a huge difference. By early evening the bulk of the packing was done, and Shane had another surprise for Parminder, a wonderful bottle of wine.

With the kids tucked into bed, exhausted after a day of labor, Shane and Parminder settled onto the couch.

"Shane, thank you you've been a wonderful help today and now this. I guess I really could use a glass of wine." Parminder said.

With that they got to talking and reminiscing, a lot about Brian but a lot about life in general too. Shane was the only friend other than Jennifer that had such an open view of the world, Parminder really enjoyed his company.

"Shane, what about your wife? I don't want to keep you." Parminder said.

"Parm, Jill and I split up about three months ago, I guess you hadn't heard." Shane replied.

"No, I hadn't, we've been so busy with things here, I'm really sorry Shane." Parminder said and gave him a hug. A hug that lingered and eventually turned into a kiss.

A Man's Touch

Parminder awoke sometime around 3am, thankfully before the children did as she found herself asleep in Shane's arms on the couch.

She knew she needed to get up and get Shane up, but she lingered. She lingered because she was enjoying the moment, enjoying a man's touch for the first time in over a year. She gave herself a few more minutes to indulge and when Indian guilt started to settle in, she woke Shane.

"Oh my God Parm, what time is it?" he said, also suddenly seeming to deal with some guilt.

"I'm so sorry, I don't know what got into me." he continued. Parminder reached up and gave him a kiss and simply said "Thank you."

They both gathered themselves and Parminder saw Shane to the door and then got to bed herself.

Not surprisingly she was visited that night in her dreams. She was young again and she was in the kitchen preparing Chai tea for a group of visitors and was a little upset because she had been planning to play with one of her friends that afternoon. Her mother came in and spoke to her "Parminder, life is not about us, life is about putting others before ourselves. You do understand don't you? You must think about Sahara and Dylan."

She awoke and understood the message from her mother. She knew she had a momentary lapse, a lapse of the flesh but sometimes the body needs what the body needs.

Later that week, while at work, Parminder and Jennifer were sitting having a tea and Jennifer asked, "So I hear Shane came over to help you pack?"

"Yes, he did and just so you know, we shared a moment." Parminder replied.

"Oh my God, I knew it, so what's going on?" Jennifer asked excitedly.

Remembering her dream, Parminder replied "Jennifer, you must understand that as an Indian woman we are subject to a different set of expectations than your culture is. Shane is a wonderful man and under different circumstances things might evolve, but you need to understand, this is not the right time."

She said it in such a manner that Jennifer got it, right away. Jennifer in all honesty simply wanted to see Parminder happy, but she understood, through her years of friendship with Parminder that it wasn't in the cards.

"Well, I'm certainly happy you had that moment." Jennifer said with a smile.

"So am I." Parminder replied with a smile, suddenly thinking back to the moment.

A Fresh Beginning

The day dawned bright and sunny, a perfect day for a new beginning. Parminder and family packed up the last of their personal items and watched the moving truck depart for their new world.

They then stood out front and had Jennifer take a family portrait, the one that would last as the memory of such an important time in their lives, horrible door and all. They knew the new owner would address that day one.

With the picture done, the kids out their last things into the car. Parminder took her own private moment and made her way down to the basement. Down to what was at one time Brian's lair, a space that still held some very difficult memories for Parminder. If she was going to close this book, she needed to address the basement in her goodbye. She made her way around the room, slowly looking and touching each of the components of the room as if trying to touch Brian's soul itself. In the end, she sat down in the middle of the room and allowed herself a short private cry.

"Parminder, where are you? It's time to go." It was Jennifer and yes, it was time to go.

"I'm down here, I'm coming." she said.

Jennifer got it, headed back to the car with the kids and patiently waited, giving Parminder the time she needed. A few minutes later, Parminder got into the car and the four of them left their first true home forever.

When they arrived at their new home, the moving truck was already there, and the men had begun the big unload.

Sahara immediately entered the house and took charge for one specific reason, the island. She had overseen the packing of it with great authority and was now doing the same with the unpacking.

Parminder and Jennifer stood in awe and watched a fourteen-year-old pushing around a group of big strong men.

"She has quite a character doesn't she?" Jennifer said to Parminder.

"Yes, she does, my brain and Brian's strong nature, quite a powerful mix it turns out." Parminder replied with a big smile.

With Sahara's management of the movers and the other three getting their things done, by sundown the truck was gone and the new house starting to look just a little like a home.

With the work done Jennifer took her leave and the three O'Malley's sat down on the couch and looked out over O'Malley island in the nook. Sahara said, with a grin, "Welcome to the new O'Malley island." and they all took a much-needed laugh.

Moments later, the doorbell rang, Parminder got up and answered the door. It was several of the neighbors, coming by to welcome them to the new neighborhood. My God she thought, what a change from Parminder's first day after her marriage at Brian's place when the door was painted with the vile words of "Go home Paki."

Before she knew it, she was in the kitchen with a number of the neighbors sharing a glass or two of wine they so graciously brought over.

The neighbors were diverse. There was an African couple, a couple of white couples, an Asian couple and yes, an Indian couple, very modern Indian couple.

Parminder had to pinch herself to make sure it was real.

Meanwhile, in the living room Sahara, with Dylan was holding court with some of the neighbor's kids over the island, the new seventh wonder of the neighborhood.

Later that night the family, exhausted but happy, all crashed in their beds. That night Sahara had a dream she was in the backyard, of the new home, and the island was out there. She was working on it and looked up at the house. Standing at the back door was her father, she waved and he smiled back, a big broad smile and nodded.

First Day Jitters

A week later, it was D Day at least from a kid's perspective. It was September and time to return to school. For Dylan and Sahara, now both fourteen, that meant grade nine. The two of them were going to be in the same class. They felt better being together, not all siblings did, but they weren't like all siblings.

Not unlike the experience they had the first night with the neighbors, Sahara and Dylan found the school and better yet their class as diverse as the neighborhood. In fact, one of the kids who had been at their home the first night was in their class and the rumor about the island was already making its way around the school.

"So, you guys are the ones with the island. So cool, can we come by and see it?" It took them exactly one day to become the coolest kids in school.

When they got home, Parminder was waiting for them. She had taken the day off given that it was the first day of school and well, a new school and all.

When the kids got home, neither one could stop talking. Not unusual for Sahara but for Dylan, it was quite something.

"Mom, can we have some of the kids over? Everyone wants to see the island." Sahara asked.

Parminder stopped and thought for a few seconds. Not out of concern or a question about having kids over, no it was a thought about the island itself and of course Brian.

She missed him, terribly and she thought about what he would say about his creation today. The odds were that he himself had never envisioned a neighborhood full of kids looking at the island with eyes wide open and begging their parents to build one too.

For Brian, the island was a private dream. In fact, it was the dream, the escape that allowed him to survive a traumatic childhood. That was something Parminder herself fully understood. She knew in her heart Brian would have been proud to know that his dream was about to become the dream of others as well.

"Of course, you guys can." She finally said with a smile.

Well, it didn't take long. Two days later, she came home from work to find Sahara, in her favorite place, holding court over the island with a bunch of classmates.

Sahara smiled at her, Parminder nodded and smiled in her heart, the family was finally at a place they had longed for and deserved.

The smile however had a small dark cloud in the corner. That was because there was one, very important person missing out on their newfound happiness, Brian.

A New Life as Usual

So, a new life as usual began. A good one, one the family needed and one that, although Parminder would never admit it, was deserved.

The kids had a new group of friends, or better yet, following. Their home somehow became the pseudo drop in center for the local kids, with the island as the center piece. Both children were performing well, to each of their potential. Sahara was on the honor roll, in fact, the top of the roll and Dylan was a solid B student.

Dylan also became a standout on the school wrestling team and Sahara, well Sahara with her God given talent to speak, she went on to become the captain of the school debate team.

For Parminder, she was well entrenched at this point at Harvard, she was becoming well known for international women's studies and was finally working on her dream, her first book.

One afternoon at work, Jennifer joined Parminder for an afternoon tea. "So, how are you and the gang doing?" Jennifer asked.

"Jennifer, we could not be happier, the move has simply changed our life. I feel like a shadow has been lifted off our lives." she replied.

She told Jennifer about the local kids and how the island was their rallying point.

"Parm, that's amazing, I'm so happy for you guys." Jennifer said and got up and hugged Parminder.

"So, your settled in now, well what about Shane?" Jennifer asked with a smile.

"Jennifer, you are very funny, sometimes I think you're more excited about the prospect than I am." She replied with a smile.

"Of course, I am Parm, we all love living vicariously through others." Jennifer exclaimed.

"To be honest, I haven't thought much about it. I guess in some ways I've traded that thought for the focus on my book." Parminder replied.

"Parm, romance versus a book, come on, I sense some avoidance here." was Jennifer's comment.

Parminder knew there was some truth in that, the memory of that night was lovely but one night was manageable, beyond that it gets complicated.

"Jennifer, I will let you know if I decide to get back on the horse as I believe you say here. As I have mentioned before, it is somewhat complicated." Parminder said.

Jennifer recognized the tone, time to move on for now, they quickly moved onto other topics.

On her way home that day, Parminder did think about Shane again, it was complicated. One of the issues was the kids. They knew Shane, but they knew him as their father's friend.

That thought reminded her she was long overdue for a letter home.

Letters Home and Other Things

So, with things going well in general it was time for Parminder to get back to the routine of her letters home, she knew she had a waiting audience back in India and well, had some good news to pass along.

The letter home covering Brian's death was very difficult to write, and she knew it was equally difficult to read for the wonderful women in the Punjab that had supported her all these years.

She had slowed the letters down in the time since Brian's passing as she needed to recover her own spirit before writing about her life again. Now however, was the time to start again. So, as had always been her tradition, she sat down at the kitchen table, Chai tea in hand with pen and paper and began writing.

While writing, she found herself falling into a bit of a trance, assisted of course by the Chai, she was back amongst the warm breezes and tall grasses. Suddenly, she felt a distinct pain in her stomach that pulled her back to reality and not in a pleasant manner. It was not the first time she had felt that pain in recent months, it was something that she knew she would need to address with her doctor at some point.

She vaguely remembered her mother dealing with something similar just before she left for her new life in Boston. She really did need to get it looked into soon, when she had the time available of course.

It wasn't long before she started getting letters back again. Wonderful letters, letters that reminded her of the role she played for so many who had no escape aside from their imagination and dreams.

Interestingly, it was also how she received updates on her own family, and she had lost connection with her siblings long ago. It seemed the family farm was doing well, both her sisters were married, each to another farming family as is appropriate in the Punjab but sadly one of her sisters had died in a farming accident. The saddest part was it took woman from her village to tell her, not her own family.

Her brothers had also married and now between them had seven children, five of which were male, working what was an expanding farm.

A piece of her would love to see home again but she also knew in her heart that would only happen at the end, and at that point she would simply be ashes.

Keeping the Island Afloat

During the next few years, the family kept themselves afloat and in difficult moments it was Sahara that bailed them out. She did so through her spirit and never ending belief in the value of family.

Parminder was happy again; the family was happy. It was not unlike what Jennifer had told her years before, the pain of Brian's loss was fading and was being replaced with good memories, for the most part. There were tough days, but Sahara was there to pull her along.

She even thought about relationships again. She thought about Shane, but that ship had sailed. He was married again, happily this time. She was happy for him and somewhat glad that he was no longer a temptation for her. He was a good man and in time she might have given in. While she knew that wasn't wrong, it would have certainly changed the island dynamics.

In the end their move helped save their lives. The new neighborhood and new school were exactly what they needed. A life in a mixed-race community where they didn't have to look over their shoulders or worried about what their front door was going to look like.

Life was sailing ahead, for all three of them.

Following in Her Mothers Footsteps

As high school was now drawing to an end for Sahara and Dylan, Sahara had been, as usual, very focused on what was next. For her there was no greater choice than following in her mother's footsteps and to attend Harvard and well, they had hit decision week for universities.

One afternoon as they all got home, the long awaited letter had finally arrived. There was much excitement and frankly a little anxiety in the house leading up to it.

Neither Sahara nor Parminder truly believed there was a risk that Sahara would not be accepted at Harvard, her application was impeccable and having a mother work there, while it did not provide any guarantee, it certainly helped. Even Dylan was excited, he loved and respected his sister and was just an emotional person at heart.

So, there they were, the great unveiling. The three of them sat around the table as Parminder, slit the letter open, teacup at the ready in case a Chai was needed and pulled out the news.

"Sahara Kaur O'Malley, it is with great pleasure we welcome you to the Harvard University of Law." she read.

Well the neighbors could have been excused for thinking there was a murder taking place at the O'Malley's, the three of them screamed and hugged each other. Such a brilliant moment for a family that had seen its fair share of difficult times.

Dylan took his leave, something about screaming women, but before he did, he gave Sahara a last big hug, he was truly proud.

"Sahara, I'm so proud of you. I know I have my opinion of Harvard and that you had options, but I love the fact that you are following in my footsteps, and I'll see you on the campus, its lovely." Parminder said and the two them sat down and chatted about the year to come.

Dylan, who had taken his leave, was not out of earshot and while tremendously excited for his sister, he suddenly reflected on his own life and where it was headed. Unlike his sister he didn't ace school and didn't have a clear vision of where he wanted to go in life. A little sadness came over him and he felt guilty. It wasn't a day for sadness, he headed to his room and his video games, something that always lightened his mood.

"Sahara, I know you've had your heart set on law for some time. I've been so caught up in the process, so forgive me, but I've never really asked what is driving you towards law?" Parminder asked, innocently, not realizing that the answer was going to sweep her off her feet. "Mom, I'll be honest I can't let go of what happened to Dad. I want to become a prosecutor and pursue those responsible." Sahara replied, with a sudden strength of conviction in her voice.

Parminder sat down, she really should have put the pieces together. It was Sahara's strength that had kept them bound together through some of the periods where Parminder herself had lost her own. Her own emotions were suddenly tangled up in a mess of Indian upbringing and new world vigilante.

In her heart she knew she wanted justice, but it wasn't the way she was brought up. Sahara's words were right but uncomfortable in some ways for Parminder.

"Mom, are you okay with that? You seem a little off." Sahara asked. Yes, she was a little off, it was not the first time, but truth was that the children, especially Sahara, were so much more observant than they were years ago. The 'I have a headache routine.' was running thin.

"Sorry Sahara, I was caught up in thinking about what you had said. I guess I never thought about the possibility, in many ways I closed that thought when we moved here." Parminder replied.

"Mom, are you okay with me pursuing this? I never asked before, I guess I just assumed you would be." Sahara asked. She was suddenly realizing that she too had never stopped to ask the question about how her mother would feel about it. She simply assumed they would all appreciate justice for their father.

She was starting, slowly, to understand the world a little better, in many ways it was not as simple as it was made out to be.

After a few seconds, Parminder looked up at Sahara, stepped forward and hugged her. "I am Sahara, I just needed a moment to process that thought. I love the fact that you want justice. I just don't want it to consume you, I've seen what that can do to people." she said.

"I understand Mom, I just feel that I had been given a gift, a gift that perhaps can help right some past wrongs." Sahara replied.

Parminder smiled and said, "We and many other people in this world could use a little more right than wrong."

A Life of Service

After he had a chance to absorb the events of the last little while and his own ambitions in life, Dylan finally decided it was time to approach his mother.

It was shortly after Sahara's acceptance to Harvard, which played on Dylan, not out of jealousy but out of reality that he also needed to find his own direction in life. He knew Harvard wasn't in the cards, in fact university was not in cards. He was at an age where he understood himself and his strengths and weaknesses, at least to a reasonable degree.

He admired his sister, everyone admired his sister. She had been given a gift from God, a blessing and while it wasn't gifted on him, he was incredibly happy it was gifted on her, but God didn't gift him with the same intellect.

No God gave him something else, the gift of physical abilities. As he grew, he went from the quiet kid that needed his sister's protection, to the guy that people would never cross. Given this, he looked at his own options and concluded that the military was the right one for him.

The reality was he was far more like his father than he was his mother, not by choice but by genetics. Once he realized that fact, his thoughts turned to a life of service as his father had done and as many O'Malley's in the past had as well.

He himself was comfortable with it, he knew serving was an honor, despite what public opinion sometimes suggested.

So, one afternoon when his mother returned from work, he sat down with her and told her about his thought.

Parminder was a little surprised but after a moment thinking about Dylan's analysis, she understood the approach.

"Mom, I'm not speaking out of school when I say I don't have the brain you and Sahara have. You are both gifted, I'm not in that way, what I have are Dads gifts. I empathize with people, connect well with them and have a strong physical body. I want to serve, it's my little way of connecting with Dads memory." Dylan quite emotionally said.

Parminder thought about it again. She knew Dylan was right, she loved him but wasn't connected in the same way she was with Sahara. They shared a brain, just as she and her mother did.

She reached out and hugged Dylan and said, "Of course I support your decision, I think it's wonderful that you want to serve and yes, it would be an honor to your father."

With that, Dylan had a smile from ear to ear, he was the emotional child and with all that had happened to the family, to him, he very much needed that support.

When Sahara got home, Parminder told her the news. Sahara walked over to Dylan and said, "So you finally told her." and the two of them high fived and hugged each other.

Parminder laughed, she was always amazed and happy about how close the two of them were.

"Okay, okay, I suggest we go out and have a nice dinner to celebrate the two of you and your choices in life." Parminder said. Both agreed.

They chose an Indian restaurant right in downtown Boston, a big night out for the family.

During dinner, Parminder told the two children about her and Brian’s first date. How Brian had taken her to an Indian restaurant but had no idea what he was doing and they all enjoyed a good laugh.

“Dad once told me he dressed up in Indian clothing when he proposed to you.” Dylan said.

Parminder paused, then smiled and said “Yes, he did, to be honest he looked good, it was a wonderful gesture.” While the dinner was intended to celebrate the future direction of the children, they ended up spending much of dinner exchanging old stories of Brian, all of them enjoying what were some wonderful memories.

With dinner complete, Parminder ordered each of them a glass of champagne and made a toast "To your future success." She said.

All the while Sahara was already thinking about justice for her father

Life on Campus

Parminder was as giddy as Sahara was for her first day at Harvard. They carpooled together and Parminder spent the entire ride giving Sahara the Harvard low down, much of which Sahara had already gathered during the summer intake program.

"Sahara, if you need any help, just call me." Parminder said as they were about to part ways.

"Mom, I think I'll be okay." Sahara said and as she did Parminder stopped and smiled "Of course you will. My apologies Sahara, I'm just so excited you're here" she said.

"I know Mom, I'll update you later." Sahara said with a smile and they parted ways.

On their way home Sahara gave her mother the low down on day one.

Sahara enjoyed her courses, in fact she devoured them. Each afternoon on their ride home, it was Sahara's turn to talk her mother's ear off, something Parminder devoured.

This was to become a wonderful mother and daughter tradition for the next four years.

A Story of Genetics

Parminder finally made time for herself and her health and got herself to the doctor.

"Mrs. O'Malley, how long have you been experiencing these pains?" the doctor asked.

"I had them fairly regularly as a child in India, but they faded somewhat as I got older." Parminder replied.

She watched as the doctor worked through her answer and then asked, "Is there a history of any of this in your family?"

Well that was an interesting question and frankly a bit of a challenging one. The medical system in the Punjab when she was younger was not quite like present day Boston, records and regularity were not a hallmark.

"To be honest doctor, we did not have the best of medical coverage growing up in northern India. I do recall my mother having something similar." Parminder said.

"What happened to your mother?" The doctor continued.

Parminder thought about the question, surely the doctor intended the question in a purely factual way, but the question hit Parminder in her soul, hard. It was another reminder that she never closed the book with her mother. Yes, she left home for a purpose and she left even at her mother's bidding, though her mother's passing, without her there would always torment her.

She collected her thoughts and replied to the doctor "Unfortunately my mother passed away. I was living here in Boston at the time and truly do not have many details."

She watched as the doctor, once again processed her response. This time she could see he considered Parminder's background and likely could see the pain in Parminder's eyes despite her doing her best to hide it.

"I understand." he said.

"Parminder, I'd like to run some tests on you. I am a little concerned, I'm not an expert in that area but I am aware of a parasite that could explain yours and your mother's condition."

As she drove home, her thoughts once again were in flight. In flight thousands of miles away to her homeland and again wished she had maintained some form of a relationship with her siblings. That opportunity had passed long ago, she had traded it in many ways to fulfill her mother's dream and somewhat her own,

Later that night, in a deep sleep she had a dream. She was back in the fields of her homeland, she was young, and she was home at her farm and was sitting out back behind her house watching her mother toil in the fields with her father and her sisters. Her mother stopped, came over and sat with her and hugged her. She said nothing, just smiled. Suddenly a group of men approached, they were carrying a wooden platform on their shoulders. As they got close, Parminder's mother got up, looked a few moments at the ground and then a few moments at the sky and then climbed on the platform and laid down. The men started to walk away with her on the platform chanting and as they did, the platform suddenly burst into flame.

Parminder awoke in a cold sweat and with a strong pain in her stomach.

Making the Military Grade

To say Dylan was excited about boot camp was an understatement. He had been training all summer to be ready for it and when the time came, he was ripping to go.

"Dylan, you are sure you are going to be okay; I would be lying if I said I wasn't nervous for you." Parminder said as she was driving him to the pickup spot.

She wanted to drop him off at the pickup spot, wanted to see him off as it would likely be eight weeks before she saw him again.

In Parminder's heart, this was the first time she and one of the family would be apart for any duration from each other in their entire lives. Sahara wanted to come too but had school to attend. She and her brother spent much of the night before on the couch looking at old pictures and then did a private review together of the island.

"Mom, I'll be okay." Dylan replied and as he did, Parminder looked over at him. He was a man now and a very solid one.

"Of course, you are, I'm just being a mother." She said.

Parminder dropped Dylan off at the pickup point and waited for him to board the bus.

So many boys, so young and all heading off to a life of military service. Parminder knew what America meant by military service.

She grew up in a part of the world that dreaded the American military as they all knew it meant military intervention. Not on behalf of the country, no that was the media program, it was on behalf of what was good for America. The problem was, no other country could spin the story like the Americans could. She hoped in her heart that Dylan would never fall into that spin.

Once on board the bus Dylan looked around. People from all over town, from so many different cultures. One thing that was different for Dylan was that this wasn't his last case option. Many of those on the bus were here because they couldn't be anywhere else.

The military in some ways starting in the 60's and every decade since then, had become the last refuge for the poor and unskilled. Dylan knew he was different and, in many ways, knew that he had an opportunity to shine, the way his sister shined. He wanted a chance to do that.

To some degree that's why he was there. Aside from honoring his father it was about his place to be the best. School was school, it was a necessity, but it was never his place in the way it was his sister's. This was his place and he knew it, he needed to stay focused.

When they arrived at camp, it was just like all the military movies Dylan had watched leading up to this. Well all except Stripes, albeit there were some parts that ironically fit in. They were assigned to units and bunks which on day one seemed somewhat fun, but the fun wore off as soon as the drill Sergeant showed up, then shit got real.

During the eight-week basic training program, Dylan shone, so much so that he caught the eye of the military hierarchy. At the end of boot camp, he was approached by the drill sergeant "Private O'Malley there are some people that want to speak to you." The drill sergeant announced, quite loudly as he entered the barracks.

"Here Sir." Dylan replied, in his trained military voice. Dylan was led to the officer's office where several men were waiting for him. He knew right away these were not regular army guys, no, these guys were different, Dylan already had that sense.

"Private Dylan O'Malley, I'm Captain Miller, special ops, we're here to talk to you about an opportunity." the man said.

Dylan was a little taken back, he was proud of his performance at the camp, but he never correlated that into anything beyond the camp.

"Yes Sir, what opportunity may that be Sir?" Dylan replied.

The man relaxed a little, "At ease son. Your performance these last eight weeks has earned you a shot at special ops, are you interested in pursuing that shot son? It's in the best interest of your country." he said.

Dylan thought about that for a moment. Given his respect for serving, the opportunity to serve in a Special Forces unit, well the thought had never crossed his mind before, he was suddenly thrilled.

"What do I need to do Sir?" Dylan answered without realizing that he had just signed up for the toughest role in the United States army.

Making the Right Contacts

Sahara, as she had always done, became well known within the Harvard law program in very short order.

Part of it was Sahara's character, part of it was Sahara's recognition that she would need to leverage the contacts she made at Harvard once she got past Harvard. In other words, when she got down to her real life's work, seeking justice for her father.

She also joined the debate club, which most law students did. It was an opportunity for potential future lawyers to go head to head against each in a safe academic world. For Sahara it was an eye opener, she had waltzed through any challengers in high school, but at Harvard she took her lumps. She found a whole different level of competition.

The reality was it was a great preparation for the road ahead and she knew it. She just hated taken her lumps, a pride thing that she knew she inherited from her father. It gave the students a chance to show off their stuff in front of the senior academic staff. Those with connections outside the school and for Sahara, those with connections in the Justice Department, exactly where Sahara wanted to be.

One night in Sahara's third year after she excelled in a debate, she was approached by one of the heads of the Law Department, Professor Killian.

He had a guest with him, DA Higgins from the Massachusetts State District Attorney's office.

"Sahara I'd like to introduce you to DA Clair Higgins." Professor Killian said. Well Sahara's eyes lit up like the fourth of July, "It's an honor to meet you DA Higgins."

Sahara replied, trying with every fiber to maintain a degree of calmness.

"Sahara, Professor Killian has been telling me about you and well, having had a chance to watch your performance tonight, I must say I'm impressed. Have you thought about a career in the Crown Prosecutors office?" DA Higgins asked.

Sahara had to pinch herself to make sure she wasn't dreaming. Had she thought about it, there wasn't a moment since she was accepted at Harvard that she didn't think about it.

"Yes, I have, it is actually my preferred route." she replied, surprised at how well she kept her composure.

"Well, that's great to hear, we have a program with Harvard that leads to an internship with the DA's office. If you're interested, I'd like to introduce you to a few people next week." DA Higgins continued.

Sahara had a simple, but incredibly meaningful two word answer, "I am."

Special Ops

When Dylan arrived at Fort Benning, he was a combination of excited and terrified. While the idea of being chosen to be amongst America's best was incredible, the reality of the process was starting to sink in.

He was working towards become a qualified Army Ranger, more specifically, the 75th Ranger Regiment an elite airborne group, the competition was going to be hell.

He knew he would be in the training for the better part of a year and he knew there was always a chance of failing out, but Dylan was unique in some ways. He had the ability to convince himself that something needed to be accomplished and it would be, he had a mental discipline far greater than anyone else he knew.

It was something his sister always said to him, 'Dylan, you're mentally tougher than any human being I know.' and if she said it, Dylan knew it was true. He also knew that failing out of Special Ops was more often than not a failing of the mind, not the body. So, as he walked through Fort Benning for the first time, he knew, he was there to stay.

Getting to the End Game

The Harvard years were some of the best for both Sahara and Parminder. They were able to share moments most days during the week, something Parminder missed with Dylan.

For Sahara while she too enjoyed them, especially the fact that she often carpooled with her mother, she was focused on the end game.

Harvard for many was the end game and Sahara respected that. She however had an overriding goal, justice for her father.

Given her personal goal she focused on achieving excellence in each of her courses, especially the law ones. Anything less than an A wasn't good enough for her. She needed A's if she had any hope of guaranteeing the job she wanted, she needed post Harvard.

Sahara had little time for extracurricular, other than debating. She made important contacts but not social ones.

Overtime her mother became somewhat concerned about her, she felt that she was missing out on part of the experience. Parminder knew the experience, she herself had experienced the Harvard years.

"Sahara, how is school going?" Parminder asked one night.

"Good Mom, straight A's and I'm finally kicking butt in debate club." she replied.

"Sahara, I'm worried you're missing out on some of the experience." Parminder said.

"What do you mean Mom?" she replied.

"Well, there are other clubs and to be honest I had thought that you would have had more friends from the school." Parminder said.

Sahara thought about it, she was nearly done her third year. What her mother had said wasn't untrue, she realized that. She was on a mission, one that did not include the luxury of social time.

"Mom, I'm just very focused on school." she replied.

"But why Sahara? I just don't want you to look back years later and feel that you missed out of what is a wonderful time in life." Parminder said.

"Mom, it's not about me, I'm doing this for Dad." Sahara said, very emotionally.

Parminder came and sat with her. She understood Sahara's comment, how could she not, Sahara learned it from her.

Duty, it was an underpinning in the Indian culture, especially for women. While Parminder had always believed that Sahara held none of the shackles of Indian heritage it was clear not that she had inherited the concept of duty.

"I understand Sahara, perhaps when you feel comfortable that you're in a good state with your plan, we could discuss all of us having a little fun together." Parminder said.

"I would like that Mom." she replied.

The Perfect Job Offer

With the contacts Professor Killian provided and with the assistance of DA Higgins, even prior to Graduating Sahara was fortunate to receive an offer for the internship with the Massachusetts State Prosecutor's office which would lead to a full-time role as an Assistant District Attorney. Things were falling into place for Sahara.

This was one of those days when Sahara finished much earlier than her mother and took the bus home. Dylan was now full time in the army, so he also wasn't home. Sahara thought she was going to explode, such great news and no one to tell.

A couple of hours later Parminder arrived home and Sahara virtually tackled her.

"Sahara what's going on?" Parminder exclaimed while extracting herself from Sahara. "Mom, I got a job offer with the Massachusetts State prosecutor's office. Mom I got it!" she screamed.

Once Sahara calmed down, they called Dylan, he had just finished his Ranger training and was awaiting assignment at Fort Benning.

They luckily got through to him, it was Sahara that started "I got it Dylan, I got it!" she screamed just as he answered.

Dylan knew immediately what she was referring to and gave a military shout from his end. After a warm catch up conversation between the three of them, they hung up and Sahara and Parminder went out to share a celebratory dinner.

Later that night, Parminder lay in bed and thoughts wandered through her head, the same thoughts she had four years ago when Sahara confessed to her why she was pursuing law.

Parminder understood and she did then but wasn't sure if she had the heart to revisit the past. She had laid Brian to rest in the ground and in her soul all those years ago. In many ways this felt like digging him up again, yes for good reason, but reason never trumped emotion.

Also, that night, Sahara fell into a deep sleep and a lucid dream, she knew the other was speaking to her again. She had inherited the gift from her mother and grandmother, a gift that was equally at times a curse. In her dream she was a full DA and was presenting a case to a judge. As she finished the judge banged his gavel and announced guilty and as she looked up the judge was her father and he had a wonderful warm grin on his face.

A Break from Routine

It was May, Sahara had landed the role she needed to, and she approached her mother.

"Mom, about having fun, I think it's about time." Sahara said.

"Well Sahara, that's great news, what should we do?" Parminder asked.

"I've been thinking about it. Here is what I suggest. Let's drive down to Fort Benning, a road trip, pick up Dylan and then hit the coast." Sahara said.

"Hmmm, that sounds like a fine idea Sahara." Parminder replied.

"Yes, I thought so too." Sahara said with a smile.

Parminder was happy to see her in a playful mood. Sahara had just undergone four of the toughest years any student could experience.

"Well, let's get on the phone Mom, see if we can find that Dylan guy." Sahara said.

They called Fort Benning and lo and behold, he was there.

"Okay brother, can you get a week off?" Sahara asked.

"For you sis and for Mom, damn straight I can." he said.

Dylan was four years in as a Special Ops Ranger and was a good one. He was finally at a point where he could take time off, at least close to when he wanted to.

"Let me put the request in and once I have a date, I'll let you guys know. Hey sis, congrats again on the gig." Dylan said.

A few days later, just after dinner, the phone rang, Parminder answered.

"Sahara, its Dylan, he got a week, May 18th!" Parminder yelled to Sahara in the living room.

Sahara joined her and the three chatted for a bit.

"Okay, so we will meet at the airport in Atlanta, rent a car and head to Hilton Head." Sahara said.

"No road trip?" Dylan asked.

"No, you're too damn far, we will meet you at the Airport in Atlanta. I'm sure you can find a way to get there mister Special Ops man." Sahara said.

"Okay, will do. Sis you never know, you might need a Special Ops brother one day." Dylan replied.

"True, we will see you in Atlanta." She said and hung up.

The two women then got on a laptop and started to build a plan.

Hilton Head

As Sahara and Parminder walked out of the airport arrivals, there stood Dylan.

"Ladies, please follow me." he said.

They did and they found themselves standing in front of a military jeep, with the top off.

"Ladies, our ride this week." Dylan said.

Sahara laughed, Parminder didn't know what to say.

"Okay, it's not a Caddy, but hey it's fun. Mom, you need to sit in the front." Dylan said.

Sahara grabbed her mother and helped her into the front seat, it was a good step up.

Once they got out of the airport area Sahara asked, "How long of a drive is it?"

"About five hours, sit back and enjoy the ride." Dylan said.

As they drove, sun shining, top down on the jeep, Parminder was suddenly transported back to the Punjab. She closed her eyes and let the wind and sun sweep her thousands of miles away. She felt like she did when her father would put a bunch of kids in an open trailer and haul them with a tractor into the center of the village. Her father would be there to sell his goods or buy materials for the next harvest. The children were free to run around with their friends. If they could scrape a few rupees between them they would secretly buy some jalebi. It was one of the few great memories she had as a child in India, that and her times with her mother.

She had originally started the idea of a vacation for Sahara's benefit, but she was just starting to realize how much she too needed it.

About three hours in, they stopped in a small town for a late lunch.

"Mom, seems to me you were enjoying the ride up front." Sahara said.

"To be honest, yes I was. It reminded me in many ways of my youth on the farm. The sensation of the sun and the wind, it brought back some fond memories." Parminder replied.

"Mom, why did we never go to India?" Dylan asked.

Parminder thought about the question. Although she was still a little lost in memories of India, she wasn't quite ready to explain. It was a reasonable question. She and Brian had discussed it a few times when the children were younger. He believed that it would be good for the children to see both their homelands. For Parminder, there was nothing left there for her.

"Dylan, it's a complicated question, perhaps for another time if that's okay with you." Parminder replied.

"Sure, you're right, this week is about having fun and I agree with Sahara, you looked like you were having some in the Jeep." Dylan replied.

With lunch done, they re-boarded the jeep and made their way to Hilton Head.

"Wow, this is really nice." Dylan said as they drove around the island.

"It truly is." Parminder replied. She did agree. She had been in America for many years and had seen so little of it. A life of duty she reminded herself.

They pulled into the Marriott Barony Beach Club and checked in.

"Mom, I got us all a two bedroom suite here, apparently they're lovely." Sahara told Parminder and Dylan during the check in.

Once they got to the room, Parminder looked around and said, "Sahara, this is wonderful."

"Mom, you go the master bedroom and Dylan and I will share the second room." Sahara said.

Dylan smiled, "Sis, you take the room, I'll bunk out here on the couch. Remember I'm a military boy." he said.

"Okay military boy, suit yourself." she replied and hauled her suitcase into the smaller bedroom.

Once settled in they made their way down to the restaurant bar.

"Can I help you folks?" the man behind the bar asked.

Parminder did a double take, the man was Irish and very handsome. The man, also did a double take, looking straight at Parminder.

The two double takes were not lost on the children. Once they got settled in they both started in on her.

"Mom, well, looks like you have a new admirer." Dylan said.

"And Mom, I think you might also be admiring him just a little too." Sahara added.

"Kids, I'm too old for that." she replied.

She did take one more look over, he turned and smiled. First the jeep ride and now a flirt, she was suddenly feeling a whole lot younger.

They shared five wonderful days together. They did beach things some days, which was not Parminder's thing, but she was willing to go along with the kids.

It was Dylan's thing. Being six foot one and cut like an Olympic athlete, Dylan was the king of the local beach stretch for a few days.

They did a few little adventures on Hilton Head, it was pretty interesting place as they found out.

By the last day, none of them wanted to leave. It was like a little mental oasis in the middle of a storm. Dylan would be headed back to action. Sahara would start a very hard internship and Parminder knew she would be back alone again but with her own batteries recharged again.

They had their final lunch and hit the road, back to reality.

Making the Grade

Sahara aced the internship; it was a ton of hours but there is something about having a powerful end goal that gave a person the fortitude to drive through challenging times. In fact, she became the darling of the office, fair, honest but tough as nails, she exemplified the qualities any district attorney's office would respect.

It wasn't long before she was made a full Assistant District Attorney.

"Mom, they made me a full ADA today. Tonight, I'll be taking you out to celebrate." Sahara announced to her mother on the phone.

Sahara had not been home much for the last few months, she simply needed to be at the office to handle the workload. All the newbies had to deal with it, in many ways it was a rite of passage.

What was difficult was while Sahara was going through this, she could equally see her mother struggle, struggle with her health. She had to get through the internship, but eventually she would have to get back to her mother.

Managing the Risk

Things were just getting worse and worse for Kieran, his new stint in Boston seemed to have no end to it.

It was that bloody woman, Brian's kid, they needed to figure out what to do with her. She was the worst kind of pain for them, smart, empowered and now she was an Assistant District Attorney. Worse than that, Kieran knew she had a bone to pick with the IRA, after all they killed her father.

Sometimes you don't know the repercussion of actions until it's too late, Kieran thought to himself. Taking her out now would be a huge exposure. Crap, they should have killed the whole family back when they had the chance.

The plan, as always, was to keep tabs on each of the risks, the potential loose ends, the ones they needed managed. They would remind them of the cause, remind them of the price of falling out of line.

They had a list, the guys that needed a tight watch. Kevin was on that list but so was good old Sarge McPhee. Someone Kieran had not thought about for some time, but one that could expose them in a big way if he had a change of heart.

The fact was McPhee was unique. He understood the cause, he was born in Ireland and was one tough and honest character. He stood up to the IRA when he was Sarge and in a bit of a showdown they came to an agreement. He wouldn't participate, but at the same time he would turn a blind eye.

That worked for years, but with the church explosion, there was going to be too much attention. A new plan was needed, so in the middle of the night, the night of the explosion, the IRA orchestrated a meeting with the top local police officials, McPhee and a few others and crafted the retirement plan.

Sarge McPhee somewhat begrudgingly agreed. The plan worked well, until now, with ADA O'Malley digging in, Kieran knew this story would be well questioned.

The big question was, how would McPhee handle it. Time to do the rounds thought Kieran. He booked a meeting with McPhee.

As Kieran sat in the dive bar, waiting for McPhee, he was to say, just a little pissed. Kieran worked his time never to wait, he like the walk in, the power role, but in this case, McPhee upstaged him.

Kieran knew, if he had an equal, it was McPhee. He had seen as much violence in his youth as Kieran had. In fact the IRA wanted him in the cause badly, but McPhee had his own view, his move to America was his way of saying screw you.

Finally, McPhee walked in. He spotted Kieran and wandered over, taking his time.

"Kieran, you can skip the formalities, we both know why I'm here, and don't bother with the intimidation, you know I'm not one of your little lads." McPhee started, intending to take the wind out of Kieran, but he meant it, he did not like the man.

"That may be McPhee, but you know what I do and I'm here to remind you that I am keeping an eye on you and others. That O'Malley woman, she's might end up digging up things we would all prefer to keep buried. You know us, you know what we are willing to do to protect the cause." Kieran spoke, very powerfully, his face very close to McPhee's.

The two men sat, sizing each other up like two great lions who suddenly realized their territories had met. Neither one having the luxury of backing down but more so, neither one wanting to give any quarter to the other.

"I hear you Kieran, but mark my words, you come for me, without reason and you'll have the fight of your life." McPhee spoke with equal intensity.

Suddenly the two men became aware that the entire bar, albeit a small crowd, had stopped what they were doing and were watching as if their show was the heavyweight championship of the world, for them, it might as well have been.

With that Kieran finished his beer, slammed the glass down on the table and waltzed his way out of the bar, eyeing down anyone who dared look at him.

As Kieran finished and waltzed out of the bar, McPhee sat back, ordered his own beer and thought about what he had done. In his heart he knew he had what it took to stand up to that man, but the decision to do so might not be the wisest.

The fact was with his wife gone, passed from cancer a couple of years ago. He was retired, no children, the value of his own life was not what it was. He knew it, maybe this was his own way of hastening his own end.

One thing he did know, if Kieran did come after him, McPhee would make sure the man paid hell for it.

As Kieran drove home, he thought about the exchange. It wasn't his typical textbook warning, but frankly, he knew McPhee pretty well and didn't expect it to be.

The funny thing was that Kieran actually respected the man. He was so used to people groveling, here was a real challenge, a man who could hold his own against Kieran. He thought how great it would be to have him as an ally, but that wasn't in the cards. He honestly hoped it didn't come down to having to take him out, strangely, he kind of liked the guy.

Earning a Reputation

For Sahara, the celebration of landing the dream job was short lived. She soon found herself buried in work at the DA's office, as all newbies did.

While Sahara came in with a high-profile resume and a Harvard pedigree, once in the office she was the new girl, research and research was what the life became about.

One afternoon DA Higgins stopped by to check on her future star. "So, how are you finding things here?" she asked.

Sahara, never one for mincing words expressed her feelings "Frankly I'm buried in research, I so want to see the inside of a court room."

DA Higgins smiled, remembering her early days, she had been full of piss and vinegar just like Sahara, it was a tough start for characters like them.

She put her arm around Sahara and said "Kiddo, we all earn our dues. We both know you're here for a reason. Trust me, earn respect and you'll see more court room than you want."

She finished with a squeeze, just as Parminder would do. Sahara truly liked DA Higgins, she looked to her as a mentor for a good reason, the woman was a true champion of justice.

So armed with a hug, a mentor and goal, Sahara knuckled down, bought her time and systemically won the respect and in many ways the admiration of many in the office, they all knew her history.

Then one afternoon at their weekly Monday role sheet meeting, DA Higgins read out a case, looked at Sahara and said, "You got this one kiddo.” Sahara never said yes or no, just smiled from ear to ear.

Bad News from the Farm

Even before Parminder listened to the message from the doctor, she knew what it would say. She had already had the dreams, her mother had been preparing her, as her grandmother likely prepared her mother, for what was to come.

"Parminder, I've reviewed your test results and have had an expert on Indian medicine also review it, we'd need to schedule you in for a follow up." the voice message said.

There it was, a simple statement but for Parminder, knowing her own background and her dreams, it was essentially a notification of death. Coming from her world, people understood it to be just that.

Parminder called the doctor back and scheduled the visit, one she was not excited about doing but one that was inevitable.

She reflected on how the eastern world took life and especially death much more in stride than the western world did. In the west people fought death virtually from the day they were born, sometimes overlooking the beauty of life along the way. In the east, life was what the creator set out for you, you played your role, enjoyed the moments you did and gave to the next generation.

When the end came, it came, no amount of fighting was going to change that, you were pleased that you had been given a role to play.

For Parminder she played her role, a wonderful one in the big picture. She had found true love, had become a symbol and icon to so many less fortunate women back in her homeland. She had raised two amazing children, one an Army Ranger and the other an Assistant District Attorney and more so, enjoyed their time together along the way.

Yes, she lost Brian along the way, but equally she had found him too, a privilege not everyone in the world had.

So, one fateful afternoon, she made her way to the doctor to hear the verdict on her own life.

"Mrs. O'Malley, I'm afraid it isn't good news." This time it was the specialist speaking. Her doctor was also there but rightly choosing to let the specialist handle the details.

"You have a parasite that is occasionally found in the part of the world where you grew up. It's likely what was the cause of your mother's death. If found early, it's treatable, however if it is left to infest, it burrows through your entire system. We have a treatment plan for you however, the outlook is not great, less than 20% chance of survival at this stage." the specialist said.

None of what the specialist told Parminder was shocking, her dreams had prepared her for it.

Kevin's End

Kieran hung up the phone and threw his best curses out there. He didn't know if he had neighbors, if he did, they had clearly made the decision to keep to themselves, a wise one, even if they didn't know it.

He knew Kevin would fall one day, the man had no real backbone. If he had Kieran would be dead that day in the church, not Brian. Well, it was just another loose end he needed to take care of.

The word from the station was that he was missing shifts, showing up drunk. These were exactly the signs Kieran watched for and when they hit, well it was time for him to hit.

He knew where Kevin drank, the IRA knew all the details of those they needed to keep a watch on. It was a dive, a hole in the wall which was always the case for cops when they really wanted to hide away, blend into the wall.

So, one night, near closing, Kieran and a couple of the boys walked in. Two regulars, one bartender and Kevin, manageable thought Kieran. They had already figured out who the bartender was, an older guy, living alone, no family, no great loss.

The two would just be collateral damage, so be it, small price for a bigger cause

Kieran shot the bartender in the chest as he walked in. He normally would do it between the eyes, but that precision would be suspicious for a robbery. The lads put bullets into the two customers, leaving Kevin standing alone.

Kieran watched as Kevin fumbled for his service revolver and quickly said "Please Kevin, no heroics, you know why I'm here, at least let yourself go out like a man." He said.

With that, Kevin stopped reaching for his gun and bowed his head, in many ways he knew it was coming.

Kieran then put three bullets into his mid-section. He then took out Kevin's gun, put it in Kevin's hand and fired off a couple of shots behind the bar.

His lads then tossed the place and emptied the register, not for the money, but to make the scene appear like a robbery.

Job done, they packed up and walked out leaving Kevin's loose end as dead as he was.

A Cold Case Reopened

Sahara did her time and she did it well, ultimately, she was a Pitbull in court and a master in researching cases. She quickly earned the respect of the DA and the whole office.

When she felt she had the right backing she approached DA Higgins.

"I'd like permission to open a cold case." Sahara said.

"Well ADA O'Malley, I think I can guess what it might be." DA Higgins replied.

It was no secret within the DA's office that Sahara was the daughter of a policeman that was murdered and a case that was never formally closed, there were still a lot of questions outstanding.

DA Higgins knew what she was getting into when she initially met with Sahara while Sahara was still at Harvard and when she made the initial DA office offer.

She knew the case and in her own opinion knew there was something foul about it. DA Higgins privately wanted to reopen it for some time, she smelled something was wrong, as many did in her office, but she needed a champion as the police force had banded together on this one and the one thing the DA needed was a relationship with the police. Enter Sahara, she could play bad cop, she was already developing a reputation as a hardnosed true justice ADA and well, she was good.

"Okay Sahara, let's talk about your father's case. As you know it's officially unsolved, which I think both of us know that's a load of crap." DA Higgins said.

"The problem is we need a strong relationship with the police. I have my suspicions about the station your father worked out of, and yes, I think the IRA has very much infiltrated that station. I believe you know George McPhee. I was just an ADA back then, but the DA's office had a good relationship when he and captain Downey were running the place, but the guy who replaced him, he's a piece of work." she continued.

"Yes, my brother and I were quite fond of the Sarge as we knew him. It wasn't love at first sight I remember being terrified of him initially, but he won us over. He had a secret drawer full of candies for kids like us." Sahara replied.

DA Higgins laughed and said, "I've heard the rumors."

"Okay, let's talk about logistics, I think you've earned the right for this and frankly I need someone like you to light a fire under that station. Now, because of the optics I can't have you lead this, so I'm going to have ADA Murray take the lead and officially you will be assisting, but I want you to be the bad cop to his good cop, you get it right?" DA Higgins said, knowing she didn't really need an answer.

"You got it boss." was all Sahara said with a great big smile.

On her way home she couldn't wait and called her mother. "Mom, we're reopening dad's case, this is finally happening, all these years of focus to get here and now I'll be able to get justice for Dad." Sahara said.

She had been very single focused, not stopping to think about her mother's feelings on it, she honestly just assumed her mom was good with it based on their last conversation.

For Parminder she knew this was what Sahara had dreamt of and she knew why. A small piece of her was hoping the case would not be opened, not because she didn't want justice, no it was because that chapter of her life closed when they sold Brian's old house and recreated themselves in their new home.

"Sahara that is certainly good news." Parminder said, trying her very best to sound genuine. She was not one for lies even little white ones in most cases however this was one of those special exceptions.

"Mom I'll be home soon, let's celebrate with a little Indian tonight." Sahara replied. Yes, a little Indian and a chai tea were certainly in order Parminder realized.

Setting Priorities

As the news got around the office about the re-opening of the O'Malley case, there was of course a lot of buzz.

In reality none of it was negative, the older ADAs quietly were hoping that was the plan when Sahara came on board. To address the issues at that station, and more importantly, the wrongs that were committed. Sahara had systemically won the respect of new and old in the office, as she was seen to be hardnosed, honest and tireless.

ADA Murray was in the group that admired Sahara, he could be considered a mid level ADA. He had been there nine years, had a good record but suffered from the 'there's nothing special about him' syndrome.

The fact was, he was good, but not exceptional and as such, didn't stand out. That was the fact of life for most people, the pool gets thinner as you near the top. So, nine years in, he accepted his lot.

There were other ADAs that frankly would have screamed bloody murder if asked to play the role ADA Higgins had just asked him to play, in his eyes, now a more mature set, he saw the vanity in that. He was there to serve in whatever capacity the office saw fit. It didn't make him a pansy, it made him a valuable employee.

"Sahara, I just wanted to set the groundwork here. This is your show and I'm here to help you find justice" ADA Murray said.

For Sahara, those words were magic to her ears. She only knew a little of ADA Murray, in general there was little to be told, he quietly did his job well.

"Thank you, as you can guess this is a life goal for me. I don't want anything to distract us from our job, regardless of family relations, justice wasn't delivered, it's our job to ensure that it is this time." Sahara replied with honest integrity.

They spent some time working out an interview plan. What they really needed was someone to talk and Sahara suddenly thought of just the right person, good old George McPhee.

Connecting with the Past

One thing Sahara remembered from her father's service days was his original sergeant, Sarge McPhee.

As a child she remembered being terrified of the man the first time she met him, he was larger than life, big beard, big hands and terrifying eyes, but a heart of gold.

Once her and her brother got to know him, they loved him. He was like a big bear for them, always had a little something special in his desk drawer for them.

She loved that they could sit on his desk and he would tell them wonderful tall tales, he was a true old school Irishman, a natural storyteller. Sahara was both excited and concerned that his name had come up in the investigation.

What had become an interesting question, was the timing of his retirement. Sahara vaguely remember that he retired some years ago but at the time she was twelve, the event and its timing was meaningless when surrounded with the other events of the time.

Now, however, she held the responsibility of investigating issues such as this and this one, stuck out suddenly like a sore thumb.

Looking at the facts, he retired the day after the church bombing, a strange decision for a man who held such a lifetime of service.

She knew she would be visiting with him soon, but this visit would be very different, there would be no special treats for either of them.

"Carole, I need you to set up a meeting for me with George McPhee, the former sergeant at Station 52 during the time of the church bombing. His information is in the file, and I'd like it sooner than later." Sahara shouted out to her assistant.

"Will do Sahara." Carole replied.

Sahara slipped back into thought, she respected the man, but she knew it was her job to be tough on him. She suddenly laughed thinking about what her father would think of her putting the screws to the man that he himself feared.

Well, Carole did her job as usual, tracked down McPhee and interestingly enough he was able to come in the next day.

Sahara knew that most people when contacted by a crown prosecutor found a million reasons to delay and sometimes needed a subpoena. The fact that he was coming in the next day spoke to a guilty conscience and or a story to tell. She suspected it was likely both and she was soon to find out just how much.

The next day, Sahara walked into the interview room and looked up to see George McPhee. The man still basically looked the same, but his face had aged.

The biggest change was his eyes, the eyes that in his prime could take a man down with a look now looked almost hollow. Something had taken the strength and power away. She suspected what it was, but that's why he was here, so they could find that out. When he looked up, something did happen to his eyes, they smiled, just as his mouth did, from ear to ear.

He stood up and hugged Sahara, the man had not lost any of his power that was for sure.

As he sat down again, he smiled once more and said, "Look at you Sahara, you are all grown up, beautiful." Sahara almost blushed, she needed to collect herself, she was a Harvard graduate prosecutor but suddenly felt twelve years old again.

"Mr. McPhee I'm glad you came in so quickly." Sahara started but was quickly cut off, "George, please call me George." George said.

"Okay, George, the reason you're here is that we are investigating the role the IRA may have played in the church bombing back in 2002 and the subsequent death of my father and the recent death of Kevin Murphy. Specific to you, we'd like to understand why you took an early retirement, the day after the church bombing. In fact, we are also investigating why it was suddenly offered to you." Sahara explained.

She waited and watched as George mentally wiggled through possible answers. She had added the death of her father knowing it would have an effect on George.

Once he composed himself, he did provide a reasonable answer, effectively the one he provided years ago, one that he no doubt had rehearsed many times.

"Sahara, the offer of early retirement had been on the table for a while, what got me to go was them Fed boys. I knew I'd be going through a real hard time with them in charge and well, my wife wanted to move out of the city and it just seemed like the right time." George replied.

Following that they discussed some of the details, how his wife was the big push. True, George did move out of town shortly after retiring, but the problem for Sahara was that his wife passed away two years ago from cancer and there was no way of confirming that.

On the way out, Sahara thanked George for coming in and offered him a business card in case he had something more to discuss. She also reminded him that he may be needed for another meeting.

"Sahara, for you my dear, anytime." George replied and then gave her a big hug again. While it was likely inappropriate, he was perhaps the only one who could get away with that, Sahara knew it.

As she walked back to her office, she thought about George's story, it technically hung together but, in her mind, a man like George would never have walked away so easily from a fight. No, there was more to the story, she knew that, and she would get to the bottom of it.

Making Amends

George McPhee knew he had done things he wasn't proud of in his life. Some of it came with the territory but the last part, not standing up after the church explosion, he knew that was wrong.

He reflected on his meeting with Sahara, what a lovely woman, so successful. He thought how proud Brian would have been of her, it nearly brought a tear to his eyes.

There are wrongs and then there are wrongs in this world he knew. Maybe he was just getting more sentimental in his old age, but what was done to Brian was on the wrong side of wrong, he knew that. At the time he had his own life and his wife to think about, but it was different now.

He also thought about that meeting with Kieran. That was what he was protecting, the cause as they liked to run about saying as if it was banner of honor, what it was, was an excuse to kill.

He came to a decision. While one action won't make up for what he had done, more so what he had allowed to be done, it was one action in the right direction, albeit quite likely the last action of his life and if it was, he knew it was a fair tradeoff.

When he got home, he found the card Sahara had given him and dialed the mobile number.

"Sahara O'Malley here." She answered.

"Sahara, its George McPhee here, I'll cut to the chase, I do have a story to tell. Can we meet, outside the office that is, there are eyes on that place." George said.

"I can come see you." Sahara replied.

George chuckled "Sahara, there are even more eyes on this place. No, we'll have to meet somewhere outside prying eyes. I'll get instructions to you, it's likely even this line is bugged so I'll say no more here, watch for my instructions." George closed with.

He then started to work out a plan.

Sahara hung up, she knew it was likely to happen, she read characters well and George was like a lot of old school Irish guys, the heart right out there on the sleeve. She also knew that what happened to her father equally affected him.

She suddenly started to think about what he had said, eyes on her and realized that yes, she probably was in a situation where there were eyes on her. In her zest for justice, perhaps she had overlooked the importance of security. Her father had, she did not want to duplicate that mistake. She knew she needed to look at the team around her when this meeting was done.

George McPhee knew, funny enough, no one was checking old school snail mail anymore, it was all about electronics now, cell phones, email and so on. So, he sent Sahara instructions in a Harvard envelope to her mother's house and left her a quick voicemail from a pay phone inside a small bar he hung out at that simply said, "Talk to your mother about the mail."

The bigger issue was going to be able to shake any tails, but he always had a standing plan for that, just in case it was needed.

Sahara, stopped by her mother's a few days later, Parminder had called to tell her she had an envelope addressed to her.

"Sahara, what's going on?" Parminder asked. She looked a little off to Sahara, but she was too caught up in the excitement of the moment to dig. She made a mental note to check in on her mother soon.

"I'm working with old Sarge McPhee, we are meeting soon, he has information on the bombing and I'm hoping on what happened to Dad as well." Sahara replied.

With that Parminder sat down, her spirit was already weary, the thought of revisiting Brian's death was difficult, but she knew this was coming. While it had taken years, she had finally made peace with it.

She understood why Sahara needed to pursue justice, but sometimes justice came at the cost greater than the value of the justice itself. In many ways, Parminder was eager for Sahara to get to the bottom of Brian's death. How could she not, but at the same time to a degree because she had made peace with the past and revisiting it meant reopening some of her own emotions.

A Clandestine Meeting

George had arranged quite an elaborate scheme. They would meet at a Gurdwara in Jamaica Plain. Sahara went to her mother's that morning, she put on one of her mother's saris, head covered.

"Sahara, you have me a bit worried, why the need for the disguise?" Parminder asked.

Sahara was already concerned about her mother and tried to alleviate her fears. "Mom, George just thinks it's best that no one from the police station sees us together." she replied.

When she left, she took her mother's car.

On George's side, he had a long standing agreement with the owner of the local pub. If he needed, George could use the back exit and take the owner's car. So that day, he stood up and announced to the bartender he needed to hit the can. He made his way to the storeroom grabbed the spare set of keys and a bag of clothes he had left there earlier in the week. He then made his way out to the private parking in the back, got in the bar owner's car and headed out, unseen.

True to his word, good old Sarge McPhee wandered into the Gurdwara shortly after 3pm. Although in a long Indian garb, he was still quite a sight.

He picked 3:00pm as he knew it would be open and would be sparse and would be the last place an IRA member would ever look.

He made his way over to Sahara and sat down beside her and handed her a file folder.

"Sahara my dear." he said with smile, "I've provided you with a list of all the known IRA team members who were active during the church explosion time as well as the local police involved, from your father's station. Please wait until you get back your mothers to open it. I've also included what I know of the process." he continued.

Sahara for her part was a bit stunned, she was expecting a bit of a story but not this.

"Sahara, for my part, I was not involved, however, I was aware and elected to turn a blind eye. I'm ready to accept whatever charges are appropriate for me. I should have stood up years ago, while your father was still alive, that's a guilt I've carried since then." he said, with a clearly heavy heart.

"There is a lot of corruption in the system and it's time that it gets cleaned up. On that point, Sahara, you need to do a proper investigation into your own team. I can tell you there are IRA friends right in your own office. I've also put a private detective's card in the package, he's a personal friend. He's more than clean, he can help you route out any risks in the office, quietly."

Sahara had already been looking at her staff, she had some concerns and was thinking the same thing.

"Thank you, George." she replied.

She then smiled, "I'm not sure I can call you George, I still remember you as Sarge. Anyway, I've had some similar thoughts, I've ordered some encrypted secured mobile phones already, thanks again." she concluded and got up to leave.

"OK, call me Sarge" he said.

George looked around at that point, realized he was suddenly a large fish out of water in the Gurdwara and quickly made his way out.

A Cause for Concern

Once back in the office and with her door closed and locked, she opened the package and began to read the material from George. As she did, a chill ran up her spine.

In her worst nightmare she could not have imagined the extent of the corruption and the extent the IRA had infested the Boston police. This was big, really big, she was going to need some help.

The next thing she did, she called the detective that George had provided, using one of the new encrypted phones DA Higgins had ordered one they open the church bombing case.

"PI Miller here." the voice that answered said.

"DA O'Malley here, George McPhee gave me your information, I think I need some of your help." she said.

"Ah yes, George gave me the background. You know the process you used with George to meet securely? Let's use that, tomorrow, 3pm, we will talk more in person." he said

"Got it." she replied and hung up.

Sahara chuckled for a moment. She had not been in a Gurdwara for years and now suddenly twice in a week. Who would have thought that would become her secured place later in life.

The O'Malley's really were not a religious family, her father, catholic by upbringing was really agnostic. He always said he had seen too much death in the name of a fictitious man in the sky. Her mother was Sikh but tended to keep her religion to herself, likely for a variety of reasons. Most likely out of the concern of racism against her and her children in the ever less tolerant America.

So, here was Sahara visiting the Gurdwara but for the wrong reasons and suddenly just a twinge of guilt crept in.

Cleaning House

The meetings with George McPhee and the information he provided really laid out a terrifying picture of things gone wrong within the police force, in particular with her father's old station.

While it seemed hard to believe, she remembered seeing the movie Serpico a few years back and realized that the world still held men who were weak of spirit and the right amount of money held sway.

What was worse was the report she got back about her own office. PI Miller outlined three clerks in the office, who were certainly on the take from the IRA and two more that had been contacted.

While Sahara had engaged the private investigator at George McPhee's recommendation, she had not expected to obtain a report so damning, as such she did not request permission from DA Higgins.

Now she had a dilemma, she knew she had to share the critical information, but she knew it could hurt her credibility to have acted independently with something so broad.

"Mike, thoughts?" Sahara asked of ADA Mike Murray while reviewing both the George McPhee and PI Miller information.

ADA Murray was speechless for a bit. The magnitude of the information was such that it would silence anyone in a law enforcement or justice role, assuming they were honest, clearly an assumption that Sahara now questioned.

Noticing the growing shock on his face, she added "Take your time, it's a lot to absorb, I know, I've had days to go through it."

Mike finally answered, a well structured analysis, that's what he was known for. "Okay, the McPhee information provides a clear list of crimes committed and by whom in that station. It's provided, in writing by a credible source who is willing to testify. We likely need to protect him, the size of this corruption is substantial and will be very press worthy. The entire DA's office will likely need to be involved in this. We face challenges on two fronts, the IRA and our own police force. I've had experience in this which is possibly one of the reasons why I was chosen for this assignment. There is a reason police refer to themselves as a brotherhood, they stand and fight for each other. It's a union, they'll band together no matter the truth" Mike said, wisely.

"On the private investigator situation, first, be ready to have your hand slapped. Though done for the right reasons, it is outside protocol and not in the spirit of the office. Okay, that said, what this reveals is surprising and concerning. There is no question this needs to be shared with the DA. You are a clear rising star here, take your lumps on this one, in the end your star won't be diminished by it." he said.

Sahara sat and listened to an honest and terrific assessment of the situation, she was getting to know Mike more and more through the process and was starting to truly like the man.

"Mike, thank you for the great advice. Let's work up a summary and present it to the DA. This is big, and yes we're going to need help, and let me say this, I love working with you, you hit it right on." Sahara said.

For ADA Murray, recognizing his place in the justice system, this type of praise was what made the job worthwhile.

A few days later, fully armed with a detailed presentation and recommendations, Sahara and Mike briefed DA Higgins.

Not unlike Sahara's briefing of Mike, the DA held a little bit of shock. Less so on the police front, while it was broader than she anticipated, it was not out of line from what she believed was happening. The issues in her own office were the bigger problem.

The DA's office was expected to be the epitome of justice and to hear the IRA had cracked the doors of the institution was hard.

"Okay, here's what were going to do. First Sahara, consider your hand slapped on the private investigator item. Next time you come to me, something like this happens again, it will be a lot more than a hand slap, we work as a team here. Okay, next, I will convene a meeting with the full DA staff. We'll outline the issues we're facing and make sure the full team is aware. This is big and I'm going to need to speak to a few people. On a personal front, the three employees in question will be immediately terminated and the two who have been approached will be put on a three month probation with a tight watch. Funny enough, I know PI Miller, I've worked with him before and his work is impeccable. I will review the details of the report, but I have little doubt as to its accuracy" she said with a very powerful authoritative voice.

As they were leaving DA Higgins looked over at Sahara and said, "Great work kid." She was filling the role Higgins had hoped she would, with gusto, she smiled as she walked back to the office even if her hand had been slapped.

Later that week, DA Higgins executed on her actions and somewhere in Boston, in an IKEA catalogue furnished apartment, Kieran cursed two names, Sahara O'Malley and George McPhee.

A Difficult Prognosis

As Parminder sat and waited for her update appointment with the doctor and more importantly the specialist, she reflected upon the dream of her mother and Brian by the riverside.

She knew what the news would be, her mother and Brian had already told her from their world, one that saw the greater plan.

She did appreciate what the doctors had been doing, it was their job of course and more than that in this case Parminder truly believed that they cared. The issue here was that they were fighting fate, there was no treatment for that.

"Mrs. O'Malley, please come in." her own doctor said.

She stepped inside to see two other people in the office, the specialist and a middle aged ethnic woman.

"Mrs. O'Malley, this is Melva, she is a grief counsellor here at the hospital." her doctor said.

He then continued with a speech Parminder was sure every doctor was trained on at medical school. "I'm afraid it isn't good news, the treatment we had you on is not working."

As Parminder knew this already it was not a surprise, but what was a surprise was the doctor's reaction to her non-reaction.

Melva was the one that understood. She was obviously of eastern background and upbringing. The doctors being western did not understand in the same way, duty and fate. It was in fact their job to battle fate with science, small victories were the best one could hope for against the backplane of a greater plan.

"I understand doctors, thank you for your efforts." she said.

They had a brief discussion around how more could have been done if it had been found earlier and a sensible conversation with Melva about grief counselling. They both recognized the children would need it. Parminder said goodbye as if leaving any other meeting and headed home.

On her way home Parminder thought about how she would tell her children. She had spent the better part of her life preparing them for their own lives. Now she was going to have to tell them that she would have to cut the umbilical cord once again and for the final time.

It would be much easier if Brian were still around, everything would be much easier if Brian were still around. She did what she could without him and most people would say she did an amazing job but as an Indian woman she was not interested in acclaim, it was about duty.

A Constant Danger

Given what was happening inside the DA's office, Kieran still had his people monitoring Sahara's movement. It was much easier of course when he had people in her office, but the bloody woman was getting advice from somewhere, damn good advice too. Kieran had an idea from where and he had a plan for him too.

Just then the phone rang, it was his master's update call. He sat down on the plain couch and looked around. It was a different place than he had rented years ago but shit, it had the same bland lack of soul look. While that was alright for his gig in Boston is wasn't right for an Irishman, as always, he missed county Kerry.

"Kieran here." he said picking up the phone using his business voice.

"Kieran, it's Conor and the boys here." said the voice at the other end. Names were fine on these calls as the IRA, like the Justice department were using encrypted phones. Otherwise it would have been as in the Tarantino movie, Mr. Black, Mr. White and so on. In some ways modern technology took away some of the creativity.

"Kieran what's going over there? I hear our little friend had our folks tossed from her office, seems she has a feed. We have an idea who, but we wanted your opinion." Conor said in his authoritarian way.

Kieran knew who it was and the failure of his face to face with him only made it more clear to him.

"It's McPhee, for certain. I met a few weeks back with him, reminded him of the agreement and his reaction convinced me that he's the leak. We have a plan to take care of him, but I need your blessing." Kieran said.

There was a pause at the other end, George McPhee was well known to Conor and the lads too. He was respected, in many ways he was one of them, but business was business and cracks needed to be filled.

"Kieran, get rid of him and damn it, get someone back into that woman's office." was the final statement of the call.

Kieran hung up and thought about it for a few seconds. He had a plan already, he worked one up with the boys right after his meeting with McPhee.

In reality he could have taken action earlier but a piece of him resisted. He liked the guy and Kieran knew better, emotion was a one way ride to the grave in his business.

He picked up the phone again and called one of his underlings. One of the things that IRA was good at was hierarchy, in reality it was not that different than any other military.

"Sean, we are going to execute the McPhee plan. We meet at the agreed place next Tuesday at 10pm, have all the boys there and ready." he said and hung up

He thought about the plan. In some ways it reflected what could be a plan against himself, little did he know how true that was.

A Place of her Own

Sahara was equally in dread of and thrilled with the idea of her own place.

The dread of course came from the fact that she was leaving her mother and the home that the three of them built in the wake of catastrophe and in doing so, created a near magical connection between the three of them for many years.

Her mother often told Sahara she had the spiritual gift that Parminder and her mother had, so no matter where they were, in the mortal world or beyond they would always be connected.

In reality, Sahara wasn't breaking new ground, her brother had done that some time ago, he was at Fort Benning or somewhere on a special ops mission.

She worried about him, but she also knew he could handle himself. She remembered the last time they met in person, she was almost shocked. He had matured so much, he had become a big solid man, a special ops military man, a long way from the boy that needed Sahara's protection.

As that thought went through her head, she had a brief vision of her family, how her father would have been so incredibly proud of both his children.

She was at that age, she knew it, it was time to cut the cord. She was entrenched in her career, it just made sense. Logical sense that is, not emotional, if she let her emotions rule, she would never leave her mother's side.

Had she been fully Indian and born in India this would have been the way until marriage and then living with the husband's family, for better or for worse.

She was grateful for where she was and her power of choice. Marriage, well that meant finding a partner, there would be time for that once justice for her father was finally realized. In many ways she was already married to that task.

One of the reasons she was so excited about the move was because Dylan was coming to help. She truly loved him but between their two schedules they rarely saw each other anymore.

She was thankful she was as busy as she was, if she wasn't, she would be missing him more. She suspected the same was true for him, something about being twins.

Dylan, always punctual showed up at their family home at 8am on the nose, a late start for a military man.

Together he and Sahara went and rented a cube van. She really didn't have much to bring, she would build her place over time. Once back at the house the three of them made quick work of the loading and headed over to Sahara's new pad.

"So, this is what an ADA can afford." Dylan said with a little grin.

The place was not the Ritz but equally wasn't the Jamaica Plain apartment Parminder started her life in Boston in.

"Hey at least I don't sleep in a bunk." Sahara replied with a smile.

The two of them had a real bond, there was the natural part of being twins, but it went further than that, they lived through a pain that no child should ever have to, having a parent killed.

Parminder as she did when the two of them were young stepped in, equally with a smile "Okay you two, we have work to do here."

It was true Sahara didn't have much, mostly clothes. They were done by early afternoon and shared a quick celebratory early dinner.

Dylan was due somewhere, somewhere he could not say of course, leaving both Sahara and Parminder a little uneasy but they were both getting used to life with a special ops man.

Dylan drove Parminder home leaving Sahara time to reflect on her place, it was okay, she truly didn't need much. This was her first baby step away from the nest and she made it a cautious step. She was only three blocks from her mother, something that was a comfort to both of them.

As she reflected, she realized that her new home had one big hole in it, a very special one for her, the island.

Connecting the Dots across the Pond

The swiftness of DA Higgins execution of the actions following the meeting with Sahara and Mike was impressive.

She was a woman of her word and one of action. As the word made its way through the office, the name IRA became common place around the water cooler. It wasn't hard for people to figure out who the three and the two were. In fact, one of the two quit three days later, the other hung on, and fought her way back to respect. She was an honest character in the end.

The idea was to make it public to make sure people in the justice community knew the consequences of dealing with the IRA and the IRA would know the consequences of screwing with justice.

She also made true on her commitment to speak with key people in the justice system about what was going on, with a degree of confidentiality given the magnitude of the issue. She booked a follow up with Sahara and Mike.

"Okay, first, brilliant work both of you. What I'm going to tell you is that this is now part of a bigger global picture. We've been in touch with the team in charge of pursuing the IRA in Ireland. It seems this cell is well known and is centered in county Kerry. I've made contact with Justice McMillian in county Kerry. Sahara I'll provide you the information, please set up an introduction call." DA Higgins said.

"I'm on it." Sahara replied.

After a few minutes of logistics, DA Higgins took her leave.

"Mike I just want to thank you again, you've been a wonder in this. For me, as you know there's a personal issue, but you've acted as if it was the same for you, when you had no reason to. I can only hope one day I can stand as equally by your side." Sahara said, showing a degree of emotion she rarely did in the office.

Mike smiled, again hearing this type of feedback is what made his day.

"Sahara, I've watched you since you came into this office. I'm not speaking out of school to say there was a bit of a buzz when we heard you were hired, knowing your father, but you've handled yourself here with grace and integrity, it's an honor to work with you." Mike replied, also a touch emotional.

Sahara actually felt like hugging him but knew better. In the end they shared the very same reason had that brought them to the DAs office, a true desire for justice.

Together, they booked a call with Justice McMillian of county Kerry.

The next day, they got on the call.

"Justice McMillian, I'm ADA Sahara O'Malley and I'm with ADA Michael Murray, it's a pleasure to speak with you." Sahara said.

"ADA O'Malley and ADA Murray, thank you for making time for this discussion, we share a common foe, and a very dangerous one at that. ADA O'Malley, without being too intrusive, I believe you are the daughter of officer Brian O'Malley are you not?" Justice McMillian asked.

"Yes, sir I am." Sahara replied.

"Okay, well one piece of what we have that is rather certain, is that your father was killed by an IRA hitman by the name of Kieran Conor. He's the primary fixer or hitman if you like for the cell active in Boston. My condolences, by all accounts your father was a good and honest man. We have Kieran in our sight hairs, but as you will see in our briefing, it's a difficult route with the IRA. In many ways, they are part of the fabric in Ireland, but we are making progress." Justice McMillian said.

This time is was Sahara's turn to fall silent. She had been so focused on finding justice, she might just have overlooked the human part of what she was doing. To hear the name of her father's killer, that struck right to the core and a flood of emotions rushed into her.

Suddenly she was thirteen again, standing in the living room of her birth home, watching her mother on the phone, in tears, sharing her father's dying seconds.

Mike got it right away, and as the good man he was, stepped in and handled the next few minutes of the call.

In the end, they agreed that Sahara would head over to meet in person with Justice McMillian. There were just some details that were better done in person, and thus was likely going to be a landmark case.

With the call done, Sahara got up, and this time did hug ADA Murray.

A Window of Opportunity

When Kieran got the news, he reacted quickly. This was the opportunity they were looking for. He picked up the phone and rang his masters.

"What is it Kieran?" Conor replied, his tone reminding Kieran of the hierarchy, the first call should be to Mick, so it had better be good. "ADA O'Malley is about to board a flight to Dublin." he said

Okay, that was good, certainly important enough to bypass hierarchy.

"Okay Kieran, which flight?" Conor replied. The okay of course providing Kieran with the unsaid approval for the hierarchy bypass.

"American Airlines 137, arriving 7am in Dublin. We believe she has a meeting with Justice McMillian, you all know him." Kieran said.

"Okay, we will take it from here, and damn it Kieran, get someone back in that bitch's office please." Conor replied and with that hung up.

Kieran sat back down again, once again on his IKEA couch and thought once again about good old George McPhee. Kieran knew he was still pulling the strings from behind the scenes. He also knew he was right that now was the time to address that loose end.

A Journey to the Homeland

For Sahara the idea of seeing Ireland struck a chord with her. A big part of it was the opportunity to travel, she had been so busy building herself that she hadn't made the time to see the world.

She knew in her heart, from the day her father died that she had a job to do and when that was done, okay, then she could enjoy life. If in the meantime travel came with the job, well there was nothing wrong with that.

Her flight landed in Dublin at 7am, the usual for west to east cross Atlantic travel. While most of the travelers were groggy, Sahara was sharp as a knife, she had a purpose, a goal which was driving her more than her body's natural need for sleep. There would be time for that when she was done.

Her meeting with Justice McMillian wasn't until 2pm. He was respectful of overseas travelers, a nice gesture but Sahara was ready to go, she knew she would have to hold her horses as her father used to say. He had also graciously offered to come meet in Dublin, so Sahara did not have to travel to county Kerry, a trip that could have been risky. While it was true that part of the gesture was gracious, the other part was Justice McMillian's concern for Sahara's safety. She was been followed by both IRA and non uniformed police from the moment of her arrival.

Being in Ireland of course drove thoughts of her father, on every corner she would see a man who could have passed for him.

Maybe him in image but not in character, for Sahara and undoubtedly Parminder and Dylan, Brian was unique.

She had time, sitting in the hotel to think about the past, and especially about her father. She loved him, he was the symbol of what a man, a father should be. He did fall from grace at one point, it was a black spot on the family's memory and honestly it had taken years for Sahara to understand it. In many ways she might never fully understand, but her father came back, she would never forget that.

The concept of addiction is very hard for anyone who has never personally experienced it. The family can stand and watch from the outside, torn apart by the pain of seeing someone they love being tormented by demons they can't see, worse yet, they can't fight, as the addict is alone in the ring.

No, in those cases the family is allocated to the sidelines watching it play out knowing that none of them are the coach, the vice is. They are just poor fans watching a losing team over and over again.

Sahara held back tears as she thought about the island and how she was the one to fix it. Her father had abandoned it, for a time, a time that would always be painful for her.

In reality, he introduced her and her brother to the idea, a wonderful idea and he did come back, to the island albeit too briefly. Which again was why she was there in Ireland.

The clock slipped up on 9am, crap still five hours to go. She was lucky enough to have been able to check into the hotel early, but sitting in a hotel room wasn't Sahara's style, so she put a jacket on and headed out to explore. It was late spring, so the weather wasn't a challenge, not much different than Boston.

She made her way through the classic sites, Trinity College, Temple bar, and of course the Guinness storehouse. She avoided the Jameson's site, out of respect to her father, and his father.

While the experience that morning was amazing, she couldn't help but feel that she was being followed. She doubled back a few times in hopes of catching someone however she never did. Either it was her imagination or those who were following her were that good. Sadly, she was to find out later it was the latter.

She ate lunch in Temple bar, absorbing some of the Irish culture, good, bad and otherwise and made her way back to the hotel for about 1pm. This gave her an hour to get her notes together, much of which had come courtesy of George McPhee. Come 2pm she was downstairs in the lobby as instructed.

A constable approached her and asked "ADA O'Malley?" She nodded, and after showing ID, he led her to a black SUV.

As they drove the other constable said to her, "Pardon the cloak and dagger miss, but we need to be sure you are safe."

Sahara said nothing, coupled with the feeling of being followed from earlier in the day she was feeling a little uneasy. Her office had strongly recommended an escort for her trip, but she rejected it thinking it unnecessary, but she was suddenly starting to rethink that.

They arrived at a Dublin court office and the constables escorted her to a meeting room.

In the room were two people, Justice McMillian and assistant Justice Edwards.

"ADA Sahara O'Malley what a pleasure it is to meet you in person, I believe you also know assistant Justice Edwards." Justice McMillian said.

"It's truly a pleasure to meet you both as well, now let's get down to business." Sahara replied in her Pitbull way.

They dialed in ADA Murray and Sahara briefed them all on the Boston scene and asked what their thoughts were on any actions.

Sahara was not surprised that both justices knew George McPhee, it seemed that man was a legend in many ways. Justice McMillian gave Sahara the layout of the IRA structure in Ireland and in particular the cell that was managing Boston. For both of them it really connected the dots.

In the end, Sahara shared the story of her father. Justice McMillian had a lot of sympathy for her, he himself had lost a brother. For something that was supposed to be a 'cause' it certainly created a lot of pain.

Justice McMillian had some additional information for Sahara in regard to her father's death.

"Sahara, as I mentioned on the phone, the man who killed your father is a man named Kieran Conor. He is a well known IRA fixer and was very active with the Boston cell years ago and likely again now. We have a plan for him and authorization to execute it once he's back here."

Hearing that name again associated with her father's death was on one hand painful, but on another provided a means to closure.

"Justice McMillian, let's keep in contact on this issue. If I can flush him back here, we will do that." she said.

In the end, they agreed on a joint course of action. That was as good a conclusion as Sahara could have hoped for. She took her leave, knowing she had a true partner across the pond.

In the Nick of Time

Sahara was thinking over the conversation she had with Justice McMillian. She was becoming more and more aware of the IRA's reach and power. She had known a little of the group growing up, they were after all in an Irish neighborhood for thirteen years, but the full extent of the group, it was quite shocking.

She was working on connecting the dots between the information from Justice McMillian who provided the head of the snake with the information from George McPhee who provided the tail so to speak, when the lights went out.

Sahara was immediately concerned, she knew of some of the IRA tactics. She grabbed her cell phone and called the number for the constable that was stationed downstairs.

No answer okay, this was really concerning. She had just packed up her bag when there was a knock on the door.

"Hotel security miss, we need to evacuate everyone." the voice said, in a northern Irish accent.

Sahara looked through the peephole, blocked, of course.

"Just a minute I'm in the washroom." she shouted back, buying herself a couple of minutes.

Think, think she kept saying to herself, she had no doubt the men at the door were IRA. She quickly moved the night table to the door, something to slow them down and she turned all the light switches off in case the power came back on, she had some advantage in the dark.

She then called 999, busy, someone was flooding their system too.

Another loud knock on the door "Miss we need you to open the door now." the voice said.

Okay, this was it, she was a black belt in Brazilian jujitsu but that wasn't so effective against guns.

Just as her level of panic started to increase there was a banging on the balcony door. Crap, she had not closed the blinds.

She turned to see her brother of all people, standing on the balcony in a harness holding another.

Sahara figured it out immediately, grabbed her bag yelled out to the men at the door "Hold on I'm coming!" and sprang out to the balcony.

Once on the balcony she immediately got into the harness and both of them leapt off the balcony and rappelled down 14 stories to the ground.

As they landed, they could see the IRA men standing on the balcony looking down in disbelief.

Dylan and another man quickly loaded Sahara into a waiting van and off they were.

"My God Dylan am I ever glad to see you, but what the hell?" Sahara blurted out.

"You didn't think I'd let my twin sister visit our homeland for the first time without me." Dylan replied with a big smile.

They hugged, Sahara still shaking. Dylan explained that he was concerned about Sahara's safety on the trip and knowing that she would never agree to being babysat,

Dylan got authority for a Special Ops assignment. They drove to a safe house and settled in for the night.

"Dylan, my brother, my savior, you really are the best." Sahara said giving Dylan another hug. As she hugged him, she reflected on how much Dylan reminded her of her father now, but she decided to keep that to herself, they'd had enough emotion for one day already.

"It's a good thing we did that rock climbing session in high school" he said referring to Sahara's ability to repel.

For his part Dylan was thankful to have had the opportunity to use his skills for something good, something really good.

"We will all stay here tonight, and we will escort you to your flight tomorrow." Dylan said.

"As for these two men, you can call this one Ace and this one Hawk, no real names in Special Ops, I'm sure you can understand." Dylan continued.

Sahara laughed "Of course not, thank you Ace and Hawk."

"We have three other men out there. Right now, they're teaching the IRA a lesson or two, you won't meet them, but I'll pass along your thanks." Dylan said.

Ace and Hawk took their leave and Sahara and Dylan took the opportunity to catch up in person, the first time in a long time.

After the talking, Sahara settled into a deep sleep. During her sleep she had a dream, her father was standing in the doorway of their old home, he was in full uniform. He was waving at Sahara and had a big smile on his face, he bowed, turned and went into the house.

A Critical Debrief

When Sahara returned back from Ireland, she knew she was in for some attention. Having the press waiting for her the next morning at the office, that was a surprise.

The DA also had security waiting for her too, there was to be no more risks in the office DA Higgins was heard saying.

She, like all new ADAs received media training when she started. Also, like all new ADAs assumed it was for some time in future. Well for Sahara, the future had arrived.

She put the situation together in her head, and when she did, she got it. Daughter of a murdered cop, now an ADA is attacked. Rumor has it, it was the IRA in Ireland while she was working with the Irish authorities in a case. She's rescued by Special Forces, shit that's great news.

She made a mental note to remind herself that being so single focused she missed something so obvious.

Once in the office, there was a standing ovation for her and she actually blushed. She was never a shy person, but the events of the last twenty four hours simply overwhelmed her emotionally.

She realized that this was going to be a reality of her role in this case, and the case she spent the last sixteen or so years pursuing.

She made her way to DA Higgins office as requested.

"Sahara, my little Pitbull, please sit, how are you doing? Damn we almost lost you." she said.

"Flustered." was Sahara's response. DA Higgins got up and came and sat beside Sahara.

"Look, let me apologize, it was terrible oversight on my part not to send an escort with you. I missed the intensity of this case as well, I'm relieved you're back in one piece." she said.

"Pretty hot for a cold case. We're going to have a detail on you and your mother until this case is done. The fact that they went after you tells us we're barking up the right tree. We're implementing some changes in procedure around the office for the next little while. We're at war now Sahara, one that we have to win." DA Higgins said.

"Speaking of war Sahara, what's this I hear about your brother and Special Forces coming to your aid? I've put him up for a citation, I owe him a depth of gratitude, Sahara you are my star here, I wouldn't normally say that but having almost lost you, well that changes the circumstances." DA Higgins said, showing emotion for the first time since Sahara had known her.

"Thank you, I guess I'm in the big leagues now." Sahara said, pulling another smile out of DA Higgins.

"My brother is Army Rangers Special Ops out of Fort Benning. I'll be honest he just showed up on my balcony, right out of a movie script. We're twins, we used to joke about our special connection, I'm not joking anymore." Sahara continued.

"Well we need to get him here when this is finished, I need to thank him personally. Okay, now down to brass tacks, I want you to take a couple days off, yes, it's an order. I need you to shake off what happened and recharge. I need you fresh, we both need to see justice done and you are the key now. Part of it is because of who you are and your father, but Sahara, you truly earned a reputation here and you will have made this office proud." DA Higgins said.

Sahara could read the honesty in her voice. "You know under any other circumstances I'd fight you on the time off, but you're right I need a couple of days to settle my head. What are we going to do about the press?" Sahara asked.

"Don't worry, Mike is out there right now, he's had a fair amount of experience with them." DA Higgins replied. Wow, Sahara was really taking a liking to the man, a true stand-up gentleman.

Once done in the DA's office, Sahara called her mother. "Mom, I need a couple of days, I'd love to come stay with you." she said to her mother.

"Sahara you have no idea how much I would appreciate that right now." Parminder replied.

As she hung up the phone, she curled over once again in intense pain.

A Wonderful Break

As Sahara settled into the couch in her mother's home, chai tea in hand, the enormity of the last month started to settle in.

In some ways, she was at heart still that schoolgirl with a dream in her head. The last forty eight hours certainly woke her up to the reality of living the dream.

She remembered the old adage 'be careful of what you wish for." She suddenly understood it a whole lot better. The truth was, even knowing what she did at this point, she would not change a thing, her father's memory was worth any hardship in her mind.

"Mom, how are you? I've been so occupied with my own affairs that I apologize I really haven't spent enough time with you lately." Sahara said.

Parminder thought for a minute, yes, life had really changed. Fifteen years ago, they were an island, they needed each other to survive. Parminder knew that it was her role to build them a raft and she did. She did it well like many parents do without realizing that one day that raft would be finished and the children would sail off the island, leaving the parents or worse the parent alone. But such is the nature parenthood. Even knowing the end game, nothing would change, it's in the genetics.

"Sahara it's a joy to see what's become of you and your brother. It's funny as a parent, you would trade endless lonely nights to see your children happy." Parminder said with her ever elegant smile and soul. She had in many ways made that trade.

Sahara was a very intelligent woman, but she still had life to live and experiences to come. She did not fully understand what her mother had said to her. It wasn't a short coming, except perhaps in terms of years lived and that wasn't necessary chronological years, life's candle burned at the pace of each one's wick. While she could appreciate most of what her mother had said, the rest she accepted in respect of her mother, her mentor, her hero.

They spent two wonderful days, catching up, sitting over the island reminiscing and emotionally remembering Brian.

The island, which once stood for Brian's failure in life, regained its role as the altar of everything that was right about family.

Brian's recovery, while the island repairs fell short with his death, brought back the spirit of the island. It was something that was never lost on Parminder, but more so, on the two children.

As they shared the wonder and openness of their memories, each carried a personal guilt for the secrets they held in the present.

The Big Leagues

Sahara was quite ready to return to work after two days. It wasn't because she needed to get away from her mother's home, quite the opposite. The last two days were a wonderful escape from the chaos she found herself prior to her break. In fact, for the first time in many months, she slept peacefully.

"Mom I can't thank you enough, this has been wonderful. I look forward to closing this case and spending some real time together." Sahara said as she was leaving.

"Yes, I do too Sahara." Parminder whispered as Sahara left, fully knowing that time was the one thing that wasn't on her side.

Back in the office, the circus outside with the Media had died down, it was after all yesterday's news now. Once inside, Sahara made her way to DA Higgins office, Mike was already there.

She quietly thanked him for handling the media as DA Higgins was on the phone. She then hung up and turned her attention to Mike and Sahara.

"Ok, that was the Mayor, we have a meeting in his office tomorrow afternoon to review our recommendation on charges. The Chief of Police for the city of Boston will be there as well. I know I don't have to tell you this, but this is big. I want you two to lock yourselves in a room today and bring me a final plan by end of day." DA Higgins instructed them, to which both said, "Yes ma'am".

On their way out the door, DA Higgins added "And welcome to the big leagues you two."

As instructed, they spent the day ironing out the details of their plan. At the end of the day, they reviewed it with the DA and got the thumbs up.

That night, Sahara had a fitful sleep which culminated in an uncomfortable dream. She was sitting on the back steps of a farmhouse; the air was hot, but there was a wonderful breeze. Her mother was dancing, alone in the yard. She stopped and smiled at Sahara but with a tear in her eye and turned towards the tall grass at the end yard and started to walk towards it.

In the dream Sahara started calling to her mother, who simply continued to walk away and make her way into the tall grass, as she did, she disappeared. Sahara, at that point was screaming for her mother and awoke in a scream. She knew what the dream meant, she started to cry and cry and cry until she fell back into sleep.

The next day, the DA's team made its way into the Mayor's office and presented the situation. Sahara took the lead and despite still having the shadow of the dream from the night before on her, shone.

"ADA O'Malley, I understand you are the daughter of Officer Brian O'Malley, my condolences. I realize that it was many years ago but the loss of any of our police force is a sad loss." the Mayor said.

He then turned to the Chief of Police, George Dover and asked for his thoughts in the situation.

"Mayor, I did have an early review of this, it's very significant, I am in agreement with the recommended actions." George replied.

He was in a difficult position. The reality was this mess continued to exist under his watch, no one doubted he had at least some knowledge of what was happening.

The police system was both a union and a political animal, change was not as easy as one would think. For that matter the Mayor himself was clearly aware his role was a democratically elected one. The police force, which always coupled with the fire department and their families and friends represented an important voting base. One wrong move here could cost him his job at the next election.

"Shit George, this is a goddamn mess, the press is already sniffing around this, you know we're going to have to do something here." the mayor said.

Sahara noted the comment and connected the dots, she had little doubt that both men wanted to do the right thing. However, she realized at that moment, a downside of democracy, their actions were so strongly influenced by interest groups, they were at risk of not taking the right ones.

It was an insight into the greater problems in America. She suddenly remembered her parents talking about similar issues with friends, especially following the tragedy of 9/11.

She brought herself back to the moment. The Mayor and the Chief of Police were in agreement with the actions, but the issue was managing the media.

Sahara and Mike were thanked for their work and excused, DA Higgins was asked to stay. Sahara and Mike took a cab back to the office.

Later in the day, DA Higgins returned to the office and came by to see Sahara.

"Great job today, we have the green light, but it needs to be coordinated with the actions in Ireland under Justice McMillian and the Mayor's communications office. So, you got to see some of the working behind the political curtain today, what do you think?" the DA asked.

Sahara thought about it for about a second and then replied, "I'll stick with justice thank you."

Coming to Terms with Life and Death

Sahara's visit was a reminder to Parminder that the discussion with her two children would be difficult. Handling death was never easy and both of them had already lost a parent.

She had in fact also received a call from Sahara about a disturbing dream, Parminder knew Sahara was connected to the spiritual world. The children needed to be told.

She herself never had that conversation with her mother, she never got the chance. A couple of years in Boston and her mother left the mortal world. Parminder to some degree never forgave herself for not being by her mother's side.

The reality was Parminder's mother hid her illness from Parminder, knowing full well that if she had divulged it, Parminder never would have left. In many ways her mother traded her life so that Parminder could have a better one. It truly reflected the eastern concept of duty and responsibility, something her children were aware of, but it was not ingrained in them. Parminder knew in her case that it might become an issue.

The other issue of course was getting the two of them together in person. With Sahara's hours and Dylan's schedule, a secret one at that, Parminder knew she would have to find a special reason to bring the three of them together.

She leveraged the 4th of July for a special family get together and as luck would have it, both her children were available.

As Parminder prepared for the gathering that day she could not help but think back to a day so many years ago, in fact in a lot of ways, a lifetime ago. It was that infamous Thanksgiving November 2002, the infamous night that started Brian's downfall and what led ultimately to his death. It wasn't really that strange for her mind to drift there, today too was a festive day across the country and today also was to deal with death.

She prepared a traditional Indian meal almost as if on autopilot. She knew better than that, she knew her mothers' hands were guiding hers now, as they did when she was a child back in the Punjab. They were guiding her now because Parminder needed it, not from a skill perspective but from a spiritual one. Her mother knew what she needed to do and was there to help her along.

Around 6pm Sahara showed up, she had the advantage of still being in Boston. Parminder never knew where Dylan was, but that was by design, it's one of the sad parts of being a parent of a Special Ops military child, you never knew where they were.

Just as Parminder was starting to wonder if Dylan would make it, he came in through the door in full army ranger dress. Parminder took one look at him and started to cry. By God, she saw so much of Brian in him. He reached over and hugged her, they had a good cry and then moved onto a happier discussion.

"Mom, Dylan and I have something to tell you, we weren't hiding it from you but just felt it was best in person." Sahara said.

Well, that certainly perked Parminder's interest.

"Well my children have their own little thing going on now." she said with a smile. "I was warned that might happen one day." she continued still with that amazing, elegant smile that the years had taken nothing away from.

"Mom when I was in Ireland, the IRA tried to take me out, which is why I now have people watching you. Dylan actually came and saved me, he set up a special ops assignment, he saved my life." Sahara said, holding Dylan's hand.

Parminder truly did not know what to say. Her head was spinning, spinning at the news of her daughter's life being threatened. Spinning from the fact she was only now finding out. Spinning from the wave of emotions of her memory of Brian and their last fateful call.

No longer able to contain it, she fell into tears, it had turned out to be a night for confessions.

"I'm dying children." was all she said.

Picking up the Pieces

"Mom what do you mean?" Sahara, as usual was the first to respond.

Parminder collected herself, she was a little annoyed that she had broken down. It was not the way she wanted to communicate such important information but maybe she too was more affected by this then she thought. Easy enough to understand, it was her own death after all.

"I've been diagnosed with a parasite, something from my childhood. It's invasive and when it hits a certain point medical science can do nothing more, it effectively binds with your internal organs." Parminder, now back in control said.

"Mom there must be something they can do." Sahara replied, the standard western response.

Yes, the world had been to the moon and back, how could a little parasite kill someone.

"Sahara, please trust when I say that there is no more that can be done. It's likely the same thing that caused my mother's death as well." Parminder said.

With that both kids understood. Sahara, with that ever working mind continued to seek answers while Dylan, with his deep emotional structure simply continued to hold his mother.

Finally, Sahara had concluded her mental assessment and asked the next relevant question, "How long do you have?"

Parminder was prepared for the question, it was a sensible one. In fact, every human born in many ways could ask the same of whatever God they prayed to.

How long God do I have as the one thing every living thing shared is death. "Six to twelve months the specialist has said." Parminder replied, her voice again filled with the elegance and class that defined her as a person despite her own pending doom. Her end may be near but that was no reason to stop being who she was.

For Sahara, the news was devastating. There sat the queen of her world, the epitome of what a mother and more than that a woman should be, only to be cut down by a simple parasite. She now understood better what her mother was telling her about experiences in life.

She was torn, for a person so in control of herself she truly didn't know what to do with herself, scream, cry or run away. So, in the end, she took her lead from her brother and simply held her mother, her hero.

After a quiet moment of reflection together, Dylan then took the lead and walked the three of them to the altar of their home, the island.

They spent the rest of the night telling stories of the past of the island and the dream itself and somewhere, somewhere in the spirit world, Brian smiled.

Shoot out at the OK Corral

George McPhee always knew the IRA would come for him one day.

He had bought a good piece of life when he managed to come to an agreement on turning a blind eye all those years ago. However, it had never sat well with him. He of all people knew the IRA, a draw was the best one could ever hope for.

What it did give him was a chance at a life for he and his wife, his true love. He was thankful she was no longer around to see what was happening.

Turning a blind eye to money collection, well one could live with that given the alternatives. The church bombing was the proverbial straw, he knew he needed to get out then and was fortunate that he was able to 'make the arrangements.'

Brian's death triggered him. It was on the wrong side of wrong especially after what happened to Brian's father. He was tormented at the time and wanted to come forward except for two issues. Fear for his wife's life, not his own and fear he would not find a champion on the justice side.

He knew he would gather the wrath of the police and worse the IRA. The real problem was that in that station it was hard to tell one from the other.

Then along came Sahara O'Malley, a champion, finally. There was a deep connection. Shit, he had served with her grandfather and father, both men's lives cut short by the IRA.

He remembered her and her brother, just little things at the time, sitting on his desk eating candy while he told tall Irish tales. She was all grown up now and a force. He smiled at that thought, the world needed more like her and less characters such as Kieran and maybe even himself.

He failed her father, he knew, the day he turned over the reins at the station. What he did in providing Sahara with the information was a small step, he knew he would face his own judgement when he met his maker.

George knew the routine that night when the lights went out and he took a look down both ends of the street. Two cars, further down the street that were not usual, not regulars in hi rural neighbourhood, clearly rentals.

Okay, two cars, likely between four and six men.

George was hoping Kieran was in the mix, he had a score to settle, it was time.

He knew they would send a couple guys to the back door and the balance would be coming in the front under some form of distraction. He knew the playbook as well as the IRA did.

The reality was that they wanted to catch him, not kill him outright, they had their methods.

What the IRA didn't know was that George didn't use the back door anymore, not since he had trip wired it with a claymore, it helped to have old friends in the military. He made his way to backdoor and armed it.

George grabbed his assortment of weapons and made his way up the gun post he had secretly built on the roof behind the chimney a number of years ago and waited.

Smoke, okay the front porch was on fire, there was the distraction. He started counting, and just about 30 seconds later the backdoor blew, the claymore taking out two poor IRA saps. If they were at the back door, they were underlings.

On queue George raised his AR15 and took aim. Thirty more seconds, two more down on the front lawn. The last guy was running the hundred yard dash to the far rental car down the street.

George raised his gun again, not at the runner, but at driver inside the car. Through the scope he saw his mark, it was Kieran. He took the time to line up the shot, it was quite a distance and his eyes and hands were not what they were in his youth. He took his shot just as the mad dasher reached the car, right through the windshield but slightly off mark, it only nicked Kieran's left ear.

As George refocused, the car with both passengers now below the dash, sped off in reverse out of range.

George made his way quickly downstairs and out the blown out backdoor, as the fire was making its way through the house.

While he watched in pain, it was he and his wife's dream home, he picked up his cell and made a critical call.

"ADA O'Malley looks like I'm might need federal protection after all. Oh, by the way, can you advise the police that there are four dead bodies on my property?" he said.

Once he hung up, he made his way to his favorite local pub.

A Tough Time for an Old Fixer

As Kieran sped along the road, blood streaming from his left ear he was seething.

"Damn it, I told them McPhee was a wily old character. Blowing the house up was the better way, this isn't going to go over well." he said to Sean, the only other survivor of the botched attack.

The fact was he wasn't really speaking to Sean, he was speaking to himself. He knew he was in trouble, this was a big failure and it was out of the scope area where they had police friends.

Kieran survived the church incident years ago. He was not so sure he would survive this one. Ironically the masters might have been more supportive of a house bombing if he hadn't screwed up with the church bombing, funny how history can come back to bite you.

Once back at his IKEA catalog apartment, he picked up his phone and made the call, the toughest one of his life.

He knew this would be the end with the IRA and quite possibly his life.

"Conor here." was the response. This time he had pre-approval for the call, in fact they were waiting.

"It's Kieran. George McPhee is still alive, he was prepared for us, took out four of our lads. No risk of us being identified, rental cars, stolen plates, the lads are not in the system, no ID on them, they'll turn up as John Does." Kieran said, in his best but slightly failing business voice.

"Shit Kieran, this is worse than the church fiasco. Maybe we should have hired George McPhee instead of you.

Okay, get your ass on a flight to Toronto tonight and be on the first flight to Dublin tomorrow, we need you out of Boston ASAP, understood?" Conor said and with that he hung up.

He thought momentarily about how, at least he was headed home to county Kerry, for how long was the question.

Conor hung up the phone, cursed and cursed again.

Then he picked up the phone again and made an important call.

"Davey, let it be known in the Kerry justice system that Kieran Conor is no longer under IRA protection." he said.

Kieran's End

"Lads, everyone ready?" the Irish ERU team leader called out to the team members over the headset while still in the ERU van on their way to their destination.

"Ready." he received from each back into his ear from the headset.

Ready, yes, they were ready, they knew this day was coming and knew their target well. The preference of course as it is always is a peaceful arrest, but they knew their target and he was no peaceful man. The team was authorized and prepared for the use of force.

Despite Kieran's history and the fact that he was well known to the authorities in Ireland, it had taken years to get to this point where an arrest warrant, one that would stick was finally issued.

The IRA did a good, no make it a great job at managing their actions and their people. They were also masters at the visibility and information around it, so while many in the law enforcement world knew the vileness of a man like Kieran, getting to the point where they had a bullet proof case, well that took years. But here they were, finally, ready to deliver justice.

As they positioned themselves around the pub, a well-known IRA friendly pub, not one of them was expecting Kieran to go along peacefully. No this was likely going to be an ugly ending.

They held their position until the pub was relatively empty. They chose the pub because of its layout and they knew Kieran would not have access to the likely weapons, traps and escapes his home certainly had and well, it also sent a message to the IRA to take him down in one of their friendly spots.

Suddenly the team leader made the call "GO!" One of the team members slowly approached the door and tossed a stun grenade in and as soon as it hit, the full team entered, split between the front and back door.

The team entering the back door were to secure the owner and kitchen staff and seal the back exit. Those entering the front door were to secure the other two patrons and execute the warrant on Kieran.

The team, front and back, executed its duty with perfection. For a moment it seemed Kieran might go quietly but that was likely due to the effects of the stun grenade. As the team approached him as he was on the floor, he suddenly regained his sense, reached into his jacket and pulled out his famous 9mm gun.

He fired one shot, which missed and in exchange he took a dozen AR15 rounds to his body, he was dead in seconds. There ended the reign of a very bad man, rightfully in his favorite pub in his beloved county Kerry, in many ways a fitting end.

With the site secured, the team leader picked up his cell phone and made a call "Chief Justice Ferguson, this is ERU team leader O'Neill, Kieran Connor has been neutralized by our team as of 10:37pm. The site is fully secure, please send in the regular cleanup crew."

Chief Justice Ferguson hung up and then made a series of very important calls.

D DAY

There was a buzz around the office, it was D Day. Even though it was 10pm at night, everyone was on high alert, not just there but at the Mayor's office as well. There were multiple communication teams waiting across the city.

In the DA's office there were multiple arrest teams, officers from remote Boston teams each armed with arrest warrants. These teams, in a synchronized manner, would be arresting dozens of people across Boston, including a number of officers and the sergeant of Brian's old station.

They were all on hold for one call, from Justice McMillian of county Kerry Ireland who was executing a similar series of actions.

The teams were all huddled in the main office area, all eyes on Sahara, she was the woman in charge, and they all knew it.

Just as the tensions were starting to creep up, the call came in. Sahara hung up the phone and shouted, "It's a go, please execute your warrants."

Most of the ADAs were still in the office, watching in wonder as the plan was being executed. This was the largest ever execution of its type in Boston at least in recent memory, it was a site to behold.

The team that was taking down the station was being escorted by the SWAT team, in SWAT vehicles. Sahara and Mike with some clerical help manned the communications center while DA Higgins was with a communications team from the mayor's office prepared for the media onslaught.

The plan was executed with perfection. There was a new sergeant put into place at the station and the Mayor advised that the Chief of Police had been fired. In the end, the Mayor did the right thing, the public would eventually decide if they agreed.

As the actions were winding down, Sahara could see DA Higgins and the communication team running frantic, she picked up the phone, despite the late hour and made a critical call.

Once that was done, she made her way over to DA Higgins to help, she knew it was time to get used to working with the Media, she was after all, in the big leagues now.

A Rare Pleasant Midnight Call

Generally, when the phone rings at 4am it's either not good news or a nuisance or both. In this case, Sahara was waiting patiently for the call and jumped on the phone as soon as it rung.

"ADA Sahara O'Malley, this is Chief Justice Ferguson of the County Kerry Court, at 10:37pm Irish time. Kieran Conor was killed in a shootout with an Irish ERU team, you are free to execute actions and warrants at your end." he said and hung up.

Now, it's somewhat unprofessional and possibly inhumane to smile at the demise of another human, but Sahara could be excused for doing so in this case. The man himself was inhuman and had in fact killed her father.

She picked up and made one final call, her mother.

"Mom, just wanted to let you know that Kieran Conor, the man who killed Dad has just been killed by Irish police. I can't say more right now, but I'll update you on the rest tomorrow." she said.

Sahara would normally not share information such as that on a mobile phone, but since she and her mother now had encrypted secured phones, she figured it was important enough to share with her mother.

Parminder hung up the phone and laid back down, she still wasn't feeling well and was heading back to the doctor later in the week, but the news was certainly welcome.

Suddenly she began to cry and cry and cry, years of pent up pain was releasing, Kieran's death didn't bring Brian back, but it brought closure and an end to the shadow that was created with his death. There were finally clear days to come.

She then fell into a deep sleep and a dream. In her dream she was back in the Punjab. She was sitting on a side of a riverbank and tossing pebbles into the water, when a breeze suddenly kicked up and it blew her scarf across the river to the far bank.

She then noticed her mother walk down the bank and pick up her scarf, she wrapped it around herself and smiled. As she did Brian also appeared from the tall grass, walked down the bank and put his arm around Parminder's mother.

They both looked at Parminder and smiled and it was Parminder's mother who spoke "Parminder my daughter, please be at ease with yourself now, you will be joining us soon enough."

With that, the dream faded and Parminder's soul felt at ease for the first time in a very long time.

Bad News for the Cause

Conor sat in his kitchen with a beer. He would normally hit the local pub but with the situation as it was, he felt a whole lot safer in his home, at least for now.

Losing the crew in Boston was bad enough, losing Kieran was really bad, losing Mick was what really worried him.

Kieran was a big loss to the cause. He was a legend and while he was in partial retirement could still be counted on for critical needs. Kieran for them all was an example of a man dedicated to the cause.

Conor was not surprised to see him go down the way he did. He wasn't the type that could spend the rest of his life in a jail cell, he chose his own ending, consistent with the way he lived his life.

Mick was who concerned Conor. While high up the ladder, he was more of a political character, less time in the field but well connected. Conor knew if there was a knock on the door, Mick had flipped.

No doubt this would be a part of the call about to happen.

Two beers down, the phone rang. Conor answered "Conor here." and the call he dreaded began.

The dread was associated with the risk of Conor himself going down and how the IRA viewed and would manage that risk.

Conor was well connected, he had been with the cause for as long as anyone and knew some of the very top people, but sometimes information comes with a cost.

"Conor, what are your thoughts on Mick?" they asked.

"I think he's a flip risk." Conor replied, fully knowing what that meant, it was a death sentence for Mick.

Although he was in custody, the IRA had the reach to pull off that job, Conor knew that. The problem with uttering those words was that if Conor were to go down, he was now guaranteed to face the same end, it was just how things worked in their business. The thought had him grab another beer.

The balance of the call was on the wrap up of the Boston activities. They also agreed to put down Sarge McPhee, just to send a message for the future, although the future in Boston, at least in the short term was in question.

Finally, Conor was put on the IRA equivalent of leave, until they decided the risks had passed and Mick was out of the way.

As he hung up the phone, he sat back and reflected. The rest of his life was not going to be easy, all because of some woman in Boston they failed to take care of when they should have.

That was the issue at its heart, he failed, that was it. There was no room for failure in the cause, no matter who you were. He knew he would have to deal with her someday.

Judgement Day

The courthouse was complete mayhem. The goal was to arraign every one of those charged in one day. The fact was, every one of them was going to plead not guilty and their cases carried over, so it was feasible to get through the lot. It included one police sergeant, nine active officers, six retired officers, one retired police captain and five IRA members.

The media made it next to impossible to get in the front door. The DA was escorted by SWAT, while the IRA was badly hurt, they weren't dead, everyone was on alert. That just made the story even more newsworthy.
Every media outlet was there and somehow suddenly they all knew everything about Sahara. She was the new media darling in town, a role she really never wanted, but it came with the job.

She was rushed through intensive media training leading to judgement day as she got coined it and had DA Higgins standing behind her all the way.

Sahara took the lead for the two cases that she personally felt attached to and she remained in the court the entire long day.

She sat front row with DA Higgins and one other special guest George McPhee. He locked eyes with single one of the accused. It had a real effect on all those from his old station.

Sahara had suggested it might be risky for him to be there, he was after all the state's key witness, but there was no keeping him away.

By the end of the day, the press had deemed her the new sheriff in town.

As they were all preparing to go, under heavily armed escort, George had a quick chat with Sahara. "Kid, I know how big this day is for you and you can’t imagine how happy I am to see it happen, but it doesn't bring your father back, and I'm so sorry that I wasn't there for him." George McPhee told Sahara.

She turned to him, gave him a hug and said "George, Sarge, you've been wonderful, I'm just so pleased you came forward, we wouldn't be here without you."

At the end of the day, she was finally able to process everything. In all the years leading up to this, she never imagined in her wildest dreams that justice for her father would come with such a significant event. Even knowing what she did, she would never have changed a thing.

Revisiting a Wonderful Past

It had been a very long few weeks for Sahara. The big take down and the media circus that followed were tough enough, knowing her mother was dying was devastating.

The cases were well in hand now. There were so many individual cases the DA's office had to bring in help from other offices. Sahara kept two cases personally, the station Sergeant and local IRA coordinator who worked for Mick. She wished she could have had Kieran in court. While she was glad he was dead, she would have loved to watch him being grilled by the daughter of the man he killed.

She was working through some details, the phone rang, it was her mother. "Sahara, I'm really not well, do you think you could come by this evening?" Parminder said.

Sahara thought about it for a couple seconds. In all the years she knew her, she had never seen her reach out for help, this was obviously serious.

"Mom, I can do better than that, I'll come right now." Sahara replied.

As soon as she got off the phone, she popped into DA Higgins office and told her what was going on.

"Sahara, please go, we've done the first arraignment. It will be months before the rest of this unfolds as you know. Mike can carry things for a bit." the DA said.

With that, she jumped in the car and called her brother, answering service of course "Dylan, not sure where you are, but we need you here, mom needs you." she said.

As she pulled up to her mom's home, the phone rang, it was Dylan "I'm at Fort Benning, I'm taking a three day leave, I'll be there in the morning." he said. Sahara thanked him and went inside.

Parminder felt terrible for calling Sahara, a piece of her wished she could take it back. In her heart it was the parents that fielded calls from their children not the other way around, but something just felt wrong inside her, she really needed her children around.

She knew Sahara would call Dylan, that was a call she didn't want to have to make. Every time she got the answering service, it just made her wonder where he was and if he was safe.

"Mom, how are you?" Sahara asked with genuine concern.

To her, her mother suddenly looked much older and with a frailty she had never seen before.

"I'm okay Sahara, I'm so glad you came. I know I don't have much time, I would like to share as much of it with you as possible. I'm sorry to ask that of you." Parminder replied.

Sahara sat and hugged her mother, "Mom, please don't be sorry, I'm the one who should be apologizing. I've been too buried in what's going on but really I should be here."

"I saw you on the news a couple of times, you're somewhat of a star these days." Parminder said with that famous smile returning.

"Ah yes, I know, I don't think I'm cut out to be a star." Sahara replied.

Sahara got her mom tucked comfortably on the couch with chai tea in hand and then went to the kitchen to prepare dinner. She made Indian and as she did, she could swear she felt someone guiding her hands. They shared a wonderful dinner and Sahara got Parminder to bed.

Once she was sure her mother was sleeping, she got on the phone and worked some magic.

The next day Dylan came through the door and as he did he picked up his mom and hugged her. Parminder suddenly felt at bliss, she had both her children there, what more could she ask for.

"It's my army hero bother." Sahara said.

"Hey, it's my TV star sister." Dylan replied as they hugged.

"Alright, I have a little surprise for both of you. Dylan don't unpack, Mom, I packed you a bag last night, come we're getting in the car." Sahara said.

As they were driving, Parminder asked where they were going. Sahara looked at Dylan, he had already figured it out.

"Mom, you'll know soon enough." Sahara said with a smile.

Parminder smiled too, it really didn't matter, she was with her children, the destination was immaterial.

As they pulled into Cape Cod, Parminder laughed, "My God Sahara, you're wonderful." she said.

"Wait Mom, you haven't seen everything yet." Sahara said while passing a wink to Dylan.

A few minutes later they pulled up to a cottage. Parminder looked over at it and laughed out loud, "Sahara you little minx, how did you do this? It's wonderful." She was referring to the fact that the cottage was exactly the one Jennifer had rented for them all those years ago after Brian's funeral.

They all got out of the car and Parminder hugged Sahara. "Mom, it wasn't easy, but you can also thank Google maps." she said.

As they got inside Sahara said, "One rule, we all cook together." After some hemming and hawing from Dylan, they all agreed.

It was mid September, and not unlike the visit many years before, Mother Nature shone on them for three days.

They shared a beautiful time together, remembering their first visit and how it helped them during the hardest time of their life.

"Mom, whatever happened to Jennifer? What she did that time was one of the most wonderful acts I've ever experienced, I think in some ways it saved us." Dylan said.

"She married and moved to the west coast, she's at Berkley now. She's happy, we keep in touch, but as is the way with life, less and less each year. Yes, what she did for us will never be forgotten." Parminder replied.

It was true, what could have been seen as a relatively small gesture, ended up being so significant for a grieving family.

Jennifer was in fact Parminder's last true friend. She remembered someone saying at work years back that you never have the same friends you had when you were ten. While due to the circumstances of her childhood, that wasn't her case, the older she got, the more Parminder still appreciated the concept.

So, they spent the last night, on the couch by the fire listening to Dylan tell tales from the vault of Special Ops including his personal favorite, rappelling fourteen floors down a hotel in Dublin.

Sahara and Dylan settled Parminder into bed and spent a little time together talking about their mother and the painful conversation of how to handle her end.

"Dylan, I've spoken with her doctor, she will be hospitalized and likely soon. I know you don't control your schedule but once she's in the hospital, she won't be coming out. I'll stay with her, but please if you get a break come by and call when you can." Sahara asked of her brother.

"Sahara, I love Mom, I'll do everything I can." Dylan replied.

With their mother resting comfortably in bed, Sahara and Dylan had some time to catch up alone.

As they sat down, Dylan handed Sahara an envelope, it wasn't sealed and on the front of the envelope it was written, Dad.

"What is this Dylan?" Sahara asked.

"It's a letter to Dad. I told him how amazing you were in obtaining justice for him, thank you. I also have a confession to make, I've been writing letters to Dad for years. I know he's gone, but I struggled emotionally with his death, more than I let on, so I started writing letters and it helped me maintain a connection with his memory. The letters helped me work through my own grief. In time they became my little escape, somewhat like Dad had his island drawing when he was a kid. This however is the last, I’m closing the file now, to coin a phrase from your world." Dylan replied.

Sahara was at a loss for words. While they were twins, their makeup was quite different. Sahara was cut in her mother’s image, born with enormous intellect and was gifted with the dreams. A connection to that other world, the spiritual one as was her mother and her mother before that.

Whereas Sahara was born with massive intellectual quotient, her brother was born with an equally massive emotional quotient and was in his father’s image. He was a man of duty and service, but he wasn't gifted with the dreams and as a result his connection with his father died that day when he was killed.

It suddenly dawned on her, she had spent the better part of sixteen years grieving in her own way, a relentless pursuit of justice for her father.

She started to cry at the realization that maybe she had abandoned her brother in her single focused cause.

"Dylan, I'm sorry, I suddenly feel like I wasn't there for you, I was so caught up in finding justice for Dad." Sahara said.

Dylan reached over and hugged her "Sis, your strength and commitment in your pursuit helped me. Watching you helped me, knowing that you would eventually find him his justice. Shit, let's not forget those times you stood up for me in school yard scraps, we all grieve in our own way and time. We're here now, a chapter closed, which is why this is my last letter." Dylan said.

Enough was said on it for the time being, they now had their mother to help. So, with that they fell into a conversation about the old school days, and plenty of much needed laughs.

The question of when Parminder would be hospitalized was answered later that night. Sahara and Dylan awoke to horrible screaming, they found they mother curled up in pain, vomiting on her bed.

While Sahara grabbed a few of her mother's things, Dylan carried her to the car. Sahara got in the driver's seat and drove like a bat out of hell to the hospital.

Parminder’s Passing

Sahara's schedule was crazy, when you take down an IRA cell you end up being in high demand.

What Sahara did wasn't about fame or reputation, it was about justice first, but more so out of respect and love for her father and about giving her mother solace in her last days. A chance to join her own mother and husband with a clear spirit.

One good thing about having delivered in the way Sahara did, it bought her the privilege of stepping away from work for as long as she wanted and that was exactly what she needed at this point. Strange how fate aligns itself at times. Yes, Sahara was exhausted but more importantly her mother did not have much time left.

For Sahara the next few weeks were spent in the hospital, at her mother's side, squeezing out every last second of time that God would permit them just as Parminder did all those years ago in that last faithful call with Brian.

In addition to sharing these moments together, this was an opportunity for Parminder to explain to Sahara what she wanted to be done upon her death.

Parminder had spent a lifetime being effectively non-religious, at least on the surface. It didn’t mean she wasn't deeply spiritual. Her Sikh spirit never left her, she just placed it quietly away that day she boarded the train for her new life.

She knew that many people found religion in their final days. Sometimes it was for the human support they need and sometimes, as the ancient Egyptians did, for hopes of a better afterlife. This was not Parminder's case, she never left her beliefs, she just recognized that they didn't outwardly fit this new world of hers. Now, as the end was drawing near it was simply time to close the loop.

"Sahara." she said, her voice lacking the power it once had but none of the grace, "You know what I've told you about the Sikh religion over the years and you know what you must do." she continued.

"I need you to commit to me that you will get my ashes to the Punjabi rivers when I pass." she said.

Sahara might have thought about protesting and telling her mother that she wasn't dying soon but that wasn't Sahara's character nor was it the relationship they had.

"Of course, I will mother." Sahara replied to which Parminder added "Please make sure your brother participates, it's important that it is both of you."
Dylan had been by when he could but being in the armed forces, especially Special Ops, limited his flexibility. While he was never as close to Parminder as his sister was, he had his father's respectful character. He called regularly, and Sahara was able to keep him in the loop. He of course would be given bereavement leave in time however that would be only after his mother passed.

So, the last three weeks of Parminder's life were in many ways some of the most wonderful she had despite what the illness was doing to her body. With Sahara by her side daily and the curse of the horrible event that shook her life effectively lifted, she was finally free to let herself go.

For Sahara this was to be the most memorable time of her life. They shared laughs, hopes and dreams and Sahara was able to tell her mother in great detail what she meant to her, a gift Parminder missed out on with her own mother.

In fact, at points, Parminder almost forgot the pain of the loss of Brian, but a part of it was always there and she knew she would see him again soon.

So, one morning, as Sahara came to the room the doctor pulled her aside. She expected this, virtually every day she walked through those front doors but expected or not the reality is nevertheless harsh. "Sahara." the doctor started "I think you know what this conversation is about." Sadly, she did.

Over the few months she had grown to appreciate the man who stood care over his mother almost as vigilantly as she did, "Yes doctor I do." she replied quietly.

"Your mother has entered her last stage, she is effectively in a morphine induced coma." he continued.

Sahara understood this, it was a not well-kept secret that when a doctor understood the end was near, morphine helped the process along.

"I understand doctor." she replied again.

While he explained that Parminder would likely not know Sahara was there, she brushed that information aside. Of course her mother would know she was there, doctors in the West had the unfortunate limitation of western medicine while Sahara now understood the bigger universal picture and the eastern world.

"Thank you doctor, for everything, you have truly been wonderful." she said after she prepared herself mentally to enter that room for the last time.

There laid the most important person in Sahara's life, her mother, her hero. Sahara knew this was going to be very hard, extremely hard. How do you let go of the most loved and cherished thing in your life? Secretly she knew she would be able to, her mother had spent a lifetime preparing her and Dylan to handle anything in life. She had the internal strength that even few men were given. That day, she would need every ounce of it.

So, there they were, mother and daughter sharing their last quiet moments together. Sahara held her limp hand and watched as the breaths systematically slowed done.

Morphine was a wonderful thing in your last moments. While it took the pain from you, it also took your consciousness and it allowed you to leave the world pain free.

So, at 1:47pm on that fateful day, Sahara felt her mother's grip return, momentarily as she exhaled her final breath. With that breath gone, Sahara became aware the two sets of eyes that had been watching over her had suddenly become three.

She took a few minutes to make her own peace with God, then picked up the phone and dialed her brother's number.

Here ends Parminder's life but not her story, it is continued in Parminder's legacy.

Made in the USA
Middletown, DE
19 December 2019

81354457R00104